TAINNA

Norma Dunning

TAINNA

The Unseen Ones * Short Stories

Douglas & McIntyre

DOUGLAS AND MCINTYRE (2013) LTD.
P.O. Box 219, Madeira Park, BC, VON 2H0
www.douglas-mcintyre.com

EDITED by Peter Midgley
TEXT DESIGN by Shed Simas/Onça Design
PRINTED AND BOUND in Canada
Printed on 100% recycled paper

Douglas and McIntyre acknowledges the support of the Canada Council for the
Arts, the Government of Canada, and the Province of British Columbia through
the BC Arts Council.

LIBRARY AND ARCHIVES CANADA CATALOGUING IN PUBLICATION

Title: Tainna = the unseen ones : short stories / Norma Dunning.
Other titles: Unseen ones
Names: Dunning, Norma, author.
Identifiers: Canadiana (print) 20200417215 | Canadiana (ebook) 20200417223 |
    ISBN 9781771622714 (softcover) | ISBN 9781771622721 (EPUB)
Classification: LCC PS8607.U5539 T35 2021 | DDC C813/.6—dc23

This book is dedicated to all of us Inuit who live beyond the tundra, we who get up and live our lives in the Southern areas of Canada.

We are Inuit no matter where we stand.

Inuttigut: We the Inuit—we are here.

Contents

Author's Note

THE STORIES AND CHARACTERS CONTAINED WITHIN THIS WORK
are fictional.

Acknowledgements

I WOULD LIKE TO THANK MY AGENT, STEPHANIE SINCLAIR, FOR seeing the value in this work and for believing that others will love reading it.

I would like to thank Anna Comfort O'Keeffe from Douglas & McIntyre for seeing the publication of this work through to the finish.

My biggest thanks goes to Peter Midgley for his humour, patience and for knowing when to hug me at the end of it all. We did it again, Peter. Ma'na my friend.

Amak

Our collision was cosmic. nothing could stop us from smashing into each other. No other object could get in the way of that hug. That first hug. We had been apart for so long. More than eleven years. Eleven years of silenced voices. No touch. No harm. No foul. I knew her voice before she took the breath that started our first phone conversation in over a decade. You never forget the voice of someone you have loved so hard. It was her, sounding nervous and far away.

The connection made it sound like she was out of the country. That brought me relief. Perhaps she was living abroad, putting an ocean between us. I remember how the tension in my shoulders eased momentarily. Several times over the last decade, I had longed to hear her voice but never wanted to be the person who dialled out first. Time lets life bloom without family members in it. It's easier that way.

"I'm old now." Her first three words reminded me what she was like. Always speaking about herself first. Not asking how I was. Never thinking of others. I thought about how the passage of time, in length and in breadth, does not mean that people change within that same span of time. I reminded her that we all were old now. All of us over the age of fifty. All of us past the middle of our middle ages. She blurted out that she had left her long-time husband two years before.

I rallied back with a happy cheer: "Good for you!" Again, the younger one comforting the older one. The one that I had always thought was so much more than me. Taller. Smarter. Prettier. Skinnier. I never hit the mark of any of the standards that she had created to measure me by. I felt childhood shame wrap itself around me like it always did when I was in her presence. There it was again, a cloak of insecurity wrapping its jagged edges around my shoulders.

She continued to talk about her ex. I let her ramble on. It wasn't that I didn't like the guy. I just knew I had to be careful around him. We each wore a mask of pretence when we were around one another. I would initiate conversations about sporting events that I had never watched, stuff that I had seen in the sport page headlines.

Words with him were always difficult. His eyes never met anyone's. He was always looking east or west of the person he was speaking to, or at a skyline that he created above their forehead. He was openly less than tolerant of my family members. I was happy that she had left someone who, I thought, had never acknowledged that she lived under the same roof as him.

Finally, she asked me, "What's new?" A hard question, especially when trying to recover from the shock of an unexpected phone call. "What's new?" puts the receiver of the question into a place of obligation, turning their life into a lineup of what was most important before they answered the phone.

I found myself wanting to say something incredible, but my mind was muddled with the details of earlier in the day when my middle son had come over to talk about wanting to leave his lovely and long-time girlfriend. This was something that I didn't want to share with Sister. There was nothing in the world I felt less like talking about than my Lance. He was not a topic to lead with. Not yet and perhaps not ever. Tenacity and trust are things that must be earned.

The only way to answer the question was to make something up, to find something that lay on the periphery of my life and bring it forward. Now was the time to find that safe spot. I talked about university and how happy I was to be there. How invigorating it was to be the old lady student in the classroom, to be around young people, to read and learn. I talked about how long I had waited to do that. I was always putting the people I loved best first. Something she had intentionally forgotten to do even though we had been raised in the same home where it was taught.

There had always been someone else who came first. Someone else who needed my attention. Bills to pay, children to raise and that eternal drive to "get ahead." Always hoping for that financial nest egg. But those eggs broke every fiscal quarter in my household. Then one day, I decided to do something that I had always dreamed of, and that dream had come true. I made myself sound like a hero on the phone. Sister cooed her approval and told me that I was brave. Perhaps I needed that reassurance.

She asked about our siblings. I had no idea how any one of them was doing. Since I started university, every one of them had dropped out of my life. I was tired of the way they made fun of me, of their lack of support. Like contestants in a reality TV show, they got voted off one by one. Staving off the rising feeling of negativity inside me, I simply told her that I had no idea.

How could someone close a door for eleven years and then expect to pop their head in and ask, "How is everyone?" I told her that these days, only me and my sons remained in each other's orbits. I had no new information to offer her.

We were about two minutes into our talk when I decided to put up the barrier. Anger came over me. Don't indulge it, I told myself. I tugged at the edges of the cloak of shame that was choking me, fighting it. I straightened my shoulders. I pulled the cloak away from my throat. She was the one who had hung up the phone eleven years ago. Who was she to be able to dial out and ask, "What's new?"

I held my ground behind the barrier. Sister seemed stuck at the other end of the phone, looking for things to talk about. Or wanting to say something but not knowing how.

Eventually, she told me that she had lost her only child, her son. Her boy, Matt, who is three months older than my Lance. She had not lost him to death, but to the divorce. I reminded her that no matter how old children are, divorce affects them in different ways. After a short silence, she remarked that she had heard that my partner and I had split up years before. I nodded and then realized she couldn't see me nodding from the other end of the line.

"Yes. The best thing we ever did for each other!" I said. I am sure she could hear the smile in my words. It's the truth—his leaving was the best thing we had ever done for each other. I smiled because I remembered the day that he left and the sadness I felt at the time. But three weeks later, an incredible sense of happiness had flooded me.

I had jubilantly gone out and bought a new queen-sized bed, scrubbed the walls, hung up all the pictures I was never allowed to show off in all the decades of our marriage. Within three weeks I had become ecstatic over the fact that one of us had had the good sense to make a change. My heart was free at last.

She returned to the subject of our siblings and I felt pressured to come up with an answer. I told her that I really didn't know any of them anymore. Once our parents had left this world, so had the one thing we had in common. There was nowhere left to go home

to. Without the parents to hold us together, the old family squab-
bles resurfaced and our relationships disintegrated. It all fell flat
like a deflated balloon. She giggled. It reminded me of being little
girls together. Laughing ourselves to sleep in the double bed that we
shared. Sometimes I missed that. The small worries and stories of
small girls. She was fun once.

She asked if I'd visit her on the next long weekend. I wanted
to, but I was afraid to. She went off on a long description of how to
find her country home. She'd left Banff and moved about two hours
away into the country, the Deep Country as she called it. I tried to
write things down, getting excited about the possibility of seeing
her. I told her I'd call her the next night with an answer. After all, I
did have obligations and I needed to arrange to take time away from
the university. We hung up. I lay in bed that night, unable to sleep.

I lay there thinking about how random all of this was and how
unsettled I'd always felt around her. I asked myself if I needed this
kind of interruption in my life again. She had always treated me
like a doll that she wanted to play with for a short time. And she was
always the one who decided when the game would end, when she
had become bored with me, and who then placed me on the shelf
for at least another decade, only to be dusted off when she felt like
playing with me again.

Years and years had passed since she had last put her plaything
aside, and the accumulation of time had taken the shine off it even
more. We had literally stopping thinking of one another . . . and
now an invitation and the expectation of an answer in the morning.

I won't go alone, I decided.

WHEN THE SATURDAY OF THE LONG WEEKEND ARRIVES, I MAKE
two of my sons jump into the car with me. Off we speed down the

highway, the open road breezing around our sense of freedom. Happy to be leaving our city and all those problems. Sister and I have talked twice a week for the last month. An ease has settled over us and we are less cautious with each other on the phone now. I am excited at the thought of being able to look at her in real life.

I wonder what she looks like. If she is still the tall, slim one. The one I always felt substandard next to. The one I envied all the days of my childhood and into early adulthood. The one who I looked to for acceptance but never felt like I received it.

Music jumbles away in my rusty old Ford. My youngest son and I sing along to the songs on the radio. After a while, we put in a CD that he compiled years before. One that he titled *Songs for a Rainy Day*. My old Ford does not have iPod outlets and we are forced into using old technology. We laugh at the choices he's selected. My youngest son always knows how to take that nervous edge off me.

My unemployed middle son has come with us to get away from his life too. He never sings out loud, but he does lip-sync all the words. Even as a little boy he never sang or whistled or hummed. My hope is that one day he just will.

A trio of excited people, approaching the unknown. The farther south we drive, the darker the clouds are across the sky. The radio mentions the possibility of sleet. We may be driving into a storm, but we keep driving, two voices singing out the words to the songs on the radio while the third nods in rhythm to the music.

I burst out laughing when "Bad Moon Rising" starts to play.

"What's so funny?" asks Lance. I tell them the story of how my mother, their grandmother, used to sing "Don't go out in your nightie!" instead of the real lyrics and how we'd laugh and laugh when she did that. All the simple fun she made for us kids. All the things she did that made us laugh. All the love she poured out onto each of us. I tell them all of that. How she filled us up with the good parts of life. My childhood memories free-wheel around on the open road.

We each have our own way of expressing our excitement as we approach the small country town where Sister asked us to meet her. She doesn't live there. She lives in the high country, thirty-five miles away in a remote trail-riding camp along the Ghost River. A speck of a place according to Google Maps. She will be our guide.

My sons leave the car first, looking for their auntie from long ago. I stay inside, telling them to text me when they find her. My heart racing. A cigarette burning yellow lines into my fingertips. I glance into the rear-view mirror and moan, thinking about how I should have pulled my hair back into a ponytail. My hair, the first thing she'll critique. That will be followed by my inflated tire tube waistline. I debate putting on lipstick. My phone pings. That's my youngest texting to tell me they've found her. Time to get out and face Sister. I wish I could turn around and head back home.

Sister is at the local grocery store on the other side of the parking lot from where I had parked. I get out of my car and put some gum in my mouth. Then I start a slow walk toward them. I see the familiar silhouette that is her. Her hair long and flowing, her slim, curvy body looking the same as it always did. I want to run and jump into her arms or wrap my hands around her eyes from behind and whisper, "Guess who?" but instead I contain myself and walk at an even slower pace, thinking about what I should say first.

I don't utter one word as I approach. She turns and falls into my arms, and the orders begin once the tears dry. "Put your car here—no, not there, here—under the trees.

"Of course, it's all right—no, you won't get ticketed. This is a small town. Everyone parks here for days on end.

"No, you don't need anything from the store. We have everything we need where we're going. The high country—you'll see."

The three of us jump into her Jeep. The seat feels so high up that I am as dizzy as the hills moving past us. The radio is on and BBC is telling us world events as we drive along. No one says anything. We listen to an announcer speaking to us in a soothing voice, telling us that children were bombed in schools in the Middle East. The emotionless tone tells us what the royal family is up to. I can't hold the silence any longer.

"I really hate BBC news. Everything sounds the same to me. Babies getting killed have the same emotion as whether or not Kate has had that baby yet."

"I've never noticed," Sister replies, reaching for the radio dial and turning it off. "Tom," she says, glancing into her rear-view mirror, "Sing us a song."

Tom grins. He's the youngest, her favourite of all my four baby boys. She fussed over him when he was a toddler. She never has even begun to like Lance. Lance represents all the things that her boy, Matt, is not. Strong. Tall. Athletic and so very handsome. She has barely acknowledged his presence in the vehicle. She has always been like that with him. Only looked at him to reprimand him, to speak stern words of discipline. We hadn't been raised that way. Children are to be disciplined through words of love and patience, not anger and finger-pointing. She lost our ways or chose to not acknowledge or absorb them.

Tom begins to tap his lap, a single beat rises and he starts, "We're drivin' on the Ghost River Road, we're driving on the Ghost River Road—Hey-ho—Where do you go when you're driving on the Ghost River Road?" Sister and I join in. Lance clears his throat and looks out the window.

His memories must be meeting up with mine somewhere along the top of the foothills. He's remembering too. All the times she laughed at him tripping as a baby. How she always brings up his failing Grade Six and goes on and on about his dropping out of high school, while bragging up her son, Matt, as though he was the only success in our family. I can feel it. Not every reunion is filled with happy memories. Each one of us must wrestle with those unhappy times. The things that we've buried in a deep hole at the back of our heads.

"Want to sing too, Lance?" I ask, hoping to break the homecoming of unhappiness we both feel. In the passenger-side mirror, I see him shake his head.

Sister deliberately raises her voice. The Ghost River Road song is drowning out the truth. Tom pipes up and tells his auntie the "Don't go out in your nightie" story. Sister turns her head toward me and says with a long sigh, "You're still not telling them the truth, are you?" Here it comes. I can feel it like I did as a kid. The question that begins to line up her verbal assault weapons. I'm about to say something when she continues, "And by the way, your hair?" She shakes her head as though she's correcting a child and pokes her right index finger into my gut. "A little bit too much of the old Pillsbury Doughboy happening there!"

She's lasted longer than the expected ten minutes. I shake my head like Lance did and turn my eyes toward the passenger mirror. I don't reply. I'll never measure up. How did we ever come out of the same womb? How did we ever exist under the same roof? There are hard things that lie in our past, as sisters. Events that I never share with my sons. I will never infect the next generation with unnecessary pain. I wish I had brought my car instead of leaving it in town. We are now her hostages.

Driving along the bumpy dirt road, Sister begins a long story about the cougars that roam the area. For now, she's let the past lie where it should stay. She is telling us everything she knows about her latest cause. I begin to remember that she always had this know-it-all air about her. I tell myself that it's been too much. Her remark about our childhood was unnecessary. Reunions are not about ruining the present. I look at her profile and wonder what has really happened to her.

Her skin is the colour and texture of burned pie crust. Her skin has always been darker than mine, yet she's the one who lies in a tanning bed once a week. I've always been a lighter shade of Eskimo. Her hair has been dyed so often that I can see how it's thinning in the front. I wonder if she still starts each day with a wire push-up bra and two Spanx camisoles. One thing that pushes her tits up and the other that sucks her guts in. Her own version of being a shape-shifter. Her eyelashes are coated in layers of mascara. Her nose remains the biggest part of her. She broke it often as a kid. I grin and can still hear our middle brother and me laughing together in the basement on a cold winter's day.

That winter's day. The day when out of boredom we ended up playing Blind Man, wrapping a scarf around our eyes to shut out the daylight. After turning themselves in a circle ten times, the blind man would jut their arms out in front of themselves, zombie-like, and go searching for the other two hidden players. Feeling only the frozen cement under our woollen socks, hearing each other's whispered snickers. We would hide behind boxes or the washing machine, or near the rack of rifles my father had attached to the wall.

It was Sister's turn that day to be the blind man and Brother had told me to not hide. He had come up with the idea of staying only inches away from her as she flailed her arms about, trying to find us. I agreed and we shifted from one foot to the other, our laughter spouting out of our noses as Sister tried to find us. Laughter spilled over from my nostrils and into my throat. Sister looked so stupid and helpless. She looked the way I usually felt around her.

I had this sense of incredible power. Brother stayed close on my heels as we darted around the basement. Then Sister did the unthinkable. In her frustration, she started to walk faster and faster and ran right into a cedar beam that held up the house. SMACK! Tears ran into the stream of blood pooling onto her thin lips. She ripped off the blindfold and screamed, "I'm telling Mom!" Upstairs she ran.

I looked at my brother. "Are we gonna be in trouble?" I asked, terrified of what our mother would do to us.

"Who cares?" Brother answered, "Wasn't it funny when she banged her nose?" We both continued to laugh as we heard her tears upstairs. That was the beginning of a long series of broken noses for Sister, something that she seemed to do every other year. Her nose was never the same as the rest of ours. The rest of us have the same Inuit nose we were born with.

I grin, remembering that boring frosty day in the basement. She glances over at me and smiles. Her well-manicured, salon-tanned hand reaches out to mine. I let my hand slide into hers. I tell myself that I haven't made a mistake by opening a door that had been shut more than a decade ago. I tell myself that right now, right here, on this bumpy old Ghost River Road, I have done something that is good. Yet the voice of caution sings around the outside of my heart, reminding me to be careful.

"Can we turn the radio back on?" I ask Sister. I'm tired of hearing my own thoughts. I'm tired of how she hasn't changed after all this time. I want to stop remembering.

WE ARRIVE AT CAMP. SISTER RESIDES IN THE ONLY DOUBLE-WIDE trailer on the property. There are trail horses here and campers, mostly drunks, who stay throughout every summer. They have tents pitched along the river and there are outhouses with showers in them. Sister is like the Queen of the Camp in her fancy trailer—it has running water, three bedrooms, a large kitchen and living room complete with satellite television. I always wonder how people can call this kind of comfort camping, but Sister is happy to have us all jump out of her Jeep and pile into her big trailer. It's comfortable, and for now she's not alone.

We stack groceries from the Jeep onto the shelves and Sister reads the kitchen clock out to us. "Wine Time!!" she shouts. It's barely past one in the afternoon.

I have never been a drinker and I don't understand Sister's announcement. If there was one thing that she hated, it was Dad's breath always stinking of booze. And now, decades later, here Sister is inviting us to drink with her, and she is as excited as a child going to a parade. I don't know what to do except to agree. We are digging tall crystal wine glasses out of the cupboards. My sons are popping beer cans and we each grab a chair and head off to the riverbank. The roar of the water makes it hard for to me hear their voices, but this is a comfortable form of deafness.

Sister and I each fill up a wine glass with the red liquid. Raise our glasses high into the air and toast our being together. We laugh. We hug each other.

It is a beautiful scene. The foothills in front of the mountains around us. The river is dappled in greens and blues. Squirrels run up and down trees while we talk about world events and the people who stay in this camp summer after summer. We laugh about different things but never bring up the past.

My sons share a past with her too, but none of us speak of it. None of us ask about her son, my nephew, my sons' cousin. The afternoon drifts past us and different camp people come along out of curiosity and introduce themselves. Everyone shakes hands with everyone. In total, there are fewer than twenty people out here in the absolute middle of nowhere. Eventually, the smell of barbeques fills the air. Lance cooks up steaks and potatoes for us. Something her boy, Matt, would never have done.

After our supper, Sister and I take our full bellies to the camp communal tipi while my sons put out the fire at the trailer. We sit with a foreign student who is visiting the camp for the summer. He talks about his home in Spain and we ask him different questions about his family. We never speak about our own but ply this young guy with a million different questions about his mom and dad and his sisters. He misses them and is happy to tell us every detail.

Sister and I are avoiding each other. Hearing about a foreign family who are far away from us makes us believe that families can get along and be strong. Makes us believe that there is a reason to return to one another. Makes us believe that this visit may be a new beginning, where old memories and fights will never appear. Makes us believe that we can be like a family in Spain.

The other campers get up to go to bed just as Tom and Lance amble into the tipi. They've brought more wine and fill up our glasses again. I can feel the tiredness that comes with the release of emotion set in. I can feel the wine making me ask myself if any of this is real.

"Ah, Sila," Sister says as Tom and Lance settle into their chairs, "when are you going to stop raising your sons in a fairyland? They're adults now and it's time for them to know what is really what." She turns to them. "Now boys, we all know your mom is busy trying to bring the Eskimo back into all of us, but she never has told you the one true story."

She starts to tell the one story I never talk about. It's Friday night and the wine helps me hear our father howl, "Get them!"

I can hear Mother pause.

"Now!" Father commands.

Small steps scurry up the stairs and we are pulled from beneath our sheets. No words are spoken. No directions are given. Silently and slowly we march down the stairs in chronological order in our wrinkled pyjamas. In step.

He is there waiting, his .303 military issue slung across his belly, his military boots squeaking on the polished floor. Waiting for us. Our firing squad of one.

He has her line us up. Starting from the left, girl, boy, boy, girl, girl, boy. Like a mini residential school where children were sorted by gender and age. We fall into place like good soldiers and are presented to him. Three boys and three girls. Sister One, Sister Two, me, Oldest Brother, Second Brother and Baby Brother. Baby Brother, who can barely stand yet, teeters. We can see the grin behind his soother.

We all look down. We barely recognize the man in military boots as our father; he is that angry and drunk. Military Boots grins at Mother and winks. Like he's sharing a secret. He flicks the barrel of the rifle in her direction, motions to her to join our squad.

"Had enough!" he manages to blurt out. The barrel of the rifle weaves around our faces. We recognize it as the weapon that supplies our winter meat.

We girls are like Mother. We don't scream unless we must. The older brothers look bored. Mother is at the end of our lineup. I glance at her. Silent tear puddles have formed over top of her mouth.

"Don't," she whispers.

The sickening sound of the .303 being cocked is his only reply. Oldest Brother steps out of the lineup and slaps a hand to his left hip.

"Well look at you, old man," he says as Military Boots sighs. "Look at you, Mister War Hero. I wish your mama could see you now!"

"Shh," comes a muffled command from Mom. "Shh. Stop! Now!"

"Aw, why Mom? Someone has to say something. I mean, really? This is how this family ends? With that dumb fucker pulling a trigger?" Oldest Brother is brave. He is nine years older than me and I am one year away from starting Grade Two.

"How many times have I watched this jackass miss a moose or graze a deer? How many times have I watched geese laugh back at him? BANG! BANG! And the geese laugh back a big AURUK! AURUK!"

My sisters and I giggle. Military Boots wobbles toward us like a newborn deer.

"Look at Bambi over here, everyone!" Oldest Brother begins to laugh. Second Brother snorts. Baby Brother claps his hands in glee and says, "AiAiAi!"

"Get back with the rest. You're who I'll kill first!" Military Boots barks his orders.

"Do it!" Oldest Brother challenges. "Do it up good, you dumb shithead! Do all of us. Come on. RAT-A-TAT-TAT! Do it!"

Military Boots swings the gun toward him, but Oldest One leaps forward, twisting the nose of the gun under his own arm. His teeth are gritted and his dark eyes flash. He knocks Military Boots flat onto his back. Military Boots is lying on the floor. Oldest One jerks the rifle hard. Father lets go and Oldest One slides the rifle across the kitchen floor.

"Get the hell to bed, old man! Or I swear to God I'll pick that thing up and ram it down your drunken throat! I'll love pulling the trigger! And you—you'll be fucking dead!" He drills the fingers of his left hand into Father's chest.

Father's arms slump to his sides and he crumples into a fetal position, then rolls onto his back. Lying there on the kitchen floor, he looks like a snow angel who can't lift its wings. He begins to apologize—drunken I'm sorry words. We all sigh in relief. It's over for now. Mother goes to him and wraps her arms around his waist. Through her salty tears and snot, she mumbles "I love yous" to the man who just tried to kill us all.

They head off together. A broken pair of lovers. A broken pair of parents. They quietly close the door to their bedroom behind themselves.

Oldest One looks at us all and laughs, "Well gang, just another Friday night around here! Let's go back to bed. Last one up the stairs gets to smell all my farts for the next week!"

We race up the stairs behind him, laughing like school kids being released for the summer. Sister Two and I share a bed. Sister One is on the other side of the room in her own bed. We crawl under our DND sheets, the starched Department of National Defense garbage, and I try to think of something else, anything else. I can't, and the full moon smiles down through our tiny bedroom window. I snuggle up to Sister Two, but she pushes me away. I see her shoulders shake with tears. I try again to cuddle her up, but she kicks me hard in the shin.

"Sister?"

"Go away. I hate everyone," she mutters as she pulls the stiff sheets over her face and flattens her back against the mattress. The DND stamp covers her forehead.

"Come over here," whispers Sister One. I go to her. She is the oldest of my sisters. The one who always makes me feel better. She cuddles me close and whispers in my ear, "Don't ever think about this. Just close your eyes."

I close them. I feel Sister One stroking my short black hair and focus on the rhythm of her hands patting my head to lull me to sleep.

I watch the expressions on the faces of my sons. I'm wondering if they believe her at all. I have let our family's worst story float into their lives on the evening air. I have let the worst story settle into their memories. I can only trust that they don't completely believe the auntie that left us for so long.

I look around at our small circle and say, "And that was the night that Auntie started to hate us all. Well, on that happy note, I'm going to bed!" There's been too much wine. Too much emotion. Too much talking about things that we cannot change. It's useless to add anything more. I glare at Sister as I walk past her. How stupid of me to have expected any sort of change.

I WAKE UP AT FOUR IN THE MORNING, LIKE ALWAYS. I STAND OUT on the deck of the double-wide with a coffee and a cigarette. I am amazed that I am still here after last night's campfire story. I remind myself that I'm leaving the day after tomorrow. I find comfort in that. I'll set the story straight with my boys on the way home. Now is not the time to reopen old wounds. Besides, Sister has her new man coming along today to look at us all. I wonder what she has told him. I only know that he is a millionaire. I only know that he is white and from the city. He will be her human shield.

Sister wakes up and joins me on the deck. Like she has always done, she scolds me for smoking. I laugh at this and tell her that reformed smokers are the worst. She reminds me that cigarettes killed our father. All I can do is sigh and say, "I still miss him."

The hardness that has always been a part of Sister appears. "Well, you'd think you'd learn something from it!" she exclaims. I grin and wonder if Sister ever learned anything from our parents. All Sister ever did was turn away from them and all the rest of us. In her mind, she was never really one of us.

We agree to cook breakfast together and as the bacon sizzles, my sons wake up and come into the big kitchen. Tom pours a coffee and announces he's going to the deck for a smoke. Sister growls and says, "Fine!" Tom nods and smiles, closes the deck doors behind him. Lance stumbles in. He says good morning, but I am the only one who replies. I am amazed at the steel door that her mind can be. The hardness that lies there, the determination that she is always right. I give Lance a morning kiss and tell him that I'm happy he's here.

After breakfast, Sister takes us to meet the horses that work this camp. There are riders coming out for the day and the horses must be readied. This isn't her job. Her job is in town, but she dives in and starts grooming the horses one by one while giving us each orders to shovel up horse poop, to put bridles onto fence posts, to get some oats or chop into bags to be slung around the horses' necks.

None of us move. We have no idea what we are to do. Instead, we stand around like statues, watching her. Control is a big part of her life. She needs to have everyone doing things on her command. She should have been in the military. She would have done well. Instead, she's a nurse who has run away from her son in the city and lives where there is no cellphone service. She's gone into hiding.

Lance walks into the horse pen and starts to stroke the neck of a speckled grey mare. Tom sits down with the camp cat called Frank, lights another cigarette and tells his auntie that Frank is the best horse in camp. I laugh and start to shovel up horse manure, telling Sister that it's loaded with worms. She strokes and strokes each horse with a soft brush. She is polishing them the way we used to polish our military floors. She is wanting them to shine for whoever is coming out today. For her, so much of life is based on appearance. The older couple who run the camp eventually come along.

"Louise," the older woman says, "What would we do without you here to take care of things for us?" My head snaps over to their conversation. What the hell is going on? Sister has changed her name. I didn't know that part. Growing up she was Amak. We all called her Ama for short. It was fitting then, but now with the changes in her life maybe a name change was required. I've been calling her Ama over the last month.

"Well, Cheryl, look at all the help I have today. This is my sister and her sons. They've come out for the weekend, like I told you they would." A round of hellos and nodding happens as we all introduce ourselves. I tell Cheryl that the horses have worms and she says that she knows. Cheryl looks like a circus clown to me. Bright red cheeks and big blue eyes, the reddest lipstick I've ever seen on a woman and bleached blonde hair that hangs in thin strands under her cowboy hat. She tells me that the animals are all scheduled for meds later that night.

The riders begin to arrive and each horse is saddled up and placed into a lineup. I feel bad for them and the way they're placed into rows like four-legged soldiers. Tourists get onto their backs and each horse plods its way out onto the worn hilly paths. They've done this route too many times. Their drooping heads look like my heart.

Amak has denied and changed the name given to her. The one that represented our long-dead auntie. The auntie who laughed easy and taught us that life was good. The one who told us that residential school was in the past and what mattered was now. The one whose name I wished I had the honour of carrying. When we head back to the trailer to wait for the arrival of the millionaire, I ask her why the name change. She just shrugs and says her new name made her life easier. I walk next to her with my head down and feel such a sadness spread over me.

"Wine Time!" shouts Sister. The clock has struck noon and again we all reach into the cupboards and take out the crystal long-stemmed glasses. The red wine from the bottle with a high-end label sloshes halfway up to the rim. Sons begin snapping beer can tabs and we tuck the fold-out chairs under our arms. Off we march down the path to the river behind Sister, who follows the path without seeing what's around her. This routine has become all too familiar. She has walked this path far too many times.

We toast the sunset from last night. The sunrise of this morning. The horses. The camp and the meds that will deworm the horses. We toast the fact that I've worn white pants to camp, something that Sister has frowned upon, making the invisible cloak of shame hang heavily off my left shoulder. I have managed to embarrass her in front of her campmates. I have managed to make her seem unsuited for deep country life. It's always been like this, though. First the hair and weight comment in the Jeep, and today she has summed up all my inadequacies in a pair of white pants. I let the comment go as we toast Sister for hosting us instead. The river shouts and dances its approval of our merriment until the sound of boots behind us breaks the mood. Everything stops. The laughter fades; even the river seems to quiet itself. It's him. It's Wilhelm.

"Well, look at all of you," he says as he walks toward Sister.

She stands up and yells from beside her chair, "Hey, Sweetie!"

Wilhelm grins and looks at all of us as though he's walked into a pow-wow. He walks to the centre of our lawn chair circle and slowly turns, looking each of us in the eye as he extends his very white hand. In his starched white shirt and white cowboy hat, he grins at each of us. I can see his reflection in his shining black cowboy boots and a belt buckle that must have cost him a small fortune. He is the kind of man who can purchase pricey belt buckles. He's not the cowboy who has earned one.

I feel his soft spongy hand squish into mine and hear that inner voice that we all carry say, "You won't get along." I sense darkness in him. One of those short kinds of men with an even shorter fuse.

"Little early in the day for the grape juice, isn't it?" he asks Sister. Sister wraps her arms around his well-trimmed neck and her polished nails send glitter into the air. He kisses her cheek a little too formally.

"A toast to Will!" shouts Tom and again all the glasses are raised and again we drink to something of little consequence.

Sister shares her wine cup with Wilhelm, then hurries off to find another folding chair. We are left alone with a stranger and now we have to talk.

"How was the ride out here, Will?" I ask. This is called the smallest of small conversations. When we are stuck and have to dig hard for something to say, we talk about present conditions or the weather or things that are of no interest to any of us. Wilhelm replies that he drives a big suv and it can take anything. He is very sure that he is the biggest fish in the little pond. His arrogance outweighs his bank account.

Sister returns with the chair. The biggest chair. The throne of all lawn chairs. The chair that takes up the most space in our riverside circle. As Wilhelm starts to sit down he looks over to her and says, "You should stop drinking the vino before noon or you'll end up looking like all of your kind. All those Husky women with their big bellies and bannock-flat asses!" He's the only one who laughs.

We fall into silence. Waiting for someone to speak. Hoping that it happens soon.

THE SUN, LIKE WILHELM'S COWBOY HAT, HAS SLANTED TO THE west and he is now into the grape juice with all of us. Although I am a sworn non-drinker, I've given up and given in. It was the only way to handle it all. The wine and the discomfort have taken on the look of a slow-moving film. I am an actress in a spaghetti western.

The mountain scenery around me makes me feel like I am sitting in a postcard. The white man in a white hat talking about the stock market and giving his friend's BMW a jump-start on the way home from his daily round of golf at the club. I sit there and think about his privilege while Sister rubs his right shoulder and tells him how kind he is.

"What a pile of crap!" I hear myself say. "What a big giant pile of entitlement! Wilhelm, you should be ashamed of yourself for even telling a story like that! Is this what your life is? Going from The Firm to The Greens and only socializing with the people in your income bracket? Really? What a stupid life!"

I hear both of my sons' sudden intake of breath. I feel Lance grab my hand. I see the O shape that is now Sister's mouth. I look around, raise my nearly empty wine glass and feel my body zig-zag as I stand up. "To assholes everywhere! Long may they live in their gated communities. Long may they pass judgment on all of us. Fuckers!"

Lance takes my arm, "Come on, Mom, you've had enough," he says evenly. "I'll take you back to the trailer."

"No, Middle One. I'm staying right here. I want to know what Wilhelm would like to toast to." I turn to Wilhelm. "Say, Will, what do you have to toast to? Rising stocks? More disparity for the marginalized? The size of your tiny white cock? What would you like to toast next?"

Sister takes my other arm. "Now, let's do as Lance says—let's go for a short nap!" I grin at her, knowing that tone of voice that made me do the things I was afraid of as a kid. That was the voice that got me to jump gullies, to steal nickel candy from Fuzzies corner store, to tell lies to our mother. I knew that voice tone always ended in trouble.

"No, Sister. I want to know what Will is going to toast to. Come on, Willy, illuminate us all!"

Wilhelm shifts his weight on his throne. He spits down toward his shiny black cowboy boots. Raises his blue eyes and says, "To Native Whores!" and bursts out laughing.

"You fuck that? What is the matter with you?" I say as my eyes weave their way to Sister's. "This is what you let sleep next to you? This is what made you walk away from your marriage and your son? This small piece of Perfect White Shit?"

I begin to walk away on my own, shaking off Lance and Sister. Shaking my head. I knew that none of this would end well.

I WALK OUT INTO THE KITCHEN. I'M SO THIRSTY. I FIND MYSELF wondering if this is what a hangover is. I've never felt this sense of grogginess before. Dirty dishes are stacked up on the kitchen counter. Supper appears to be over. They ate without me. My head aches, but I still remember the words I said. I don't regret them. My problem now is that I don't have a vehicle to drive myself out of here. I need to find Ama's keys. Drive back to town and get into my own car. I must leave before things get any worse.

She never understood it. Never thought about why the things that happened growing up were the way they were. She never thought what made our folks be the people they were. She never talked to them. She never saw them in their older years. The gentleness that came to them. The peace they had found with one another. She only hated all of us and left home as soon as she could.

She had said in different phone conversations that she has no memory of growing up. It was only pain and one wrongdoing after another that befell her. She doesn't acknowledge that time. Life has only ever been about her and her and her. The sins of the father do visit the daughter, and now she doesn't have her son either. She only has white Wilhelm and his pretend life. She's in a mess.

I start going through her purse. Wallet, prescriptions for drugs I can't pronounce, gum, old after-dinner mints. No keys. I hear our younger brother in my head saying, "No Key, No mail!"—his announcement every time I lost the post office key when we were kids. I giggle quietly at the sound of his voice, coming to me here in this jailhouse.

"Sila?" I turn at the sound of my name and there she stands. Her left eye is turning purple. I gasp and go to her. I hug her hard.

She pushes me back and tells me that I have to leave.

"Amak, no. I have to stay. He did this to you!" I turn and head toward their bedroom. "I'll kill him. I swear I'll slice his lily-white nuts in half. Right here. Right now!" She grabs my arm tight and spins me around.

"You have to leave now. Here are your keys. He drove me to town to pick up your car and that's when he did this. Right there in the parking lot. Get outta here! Don't ever come back—you hear me?"

I can't stop myself from saying it. I stare hard at her and say, "Well, at least he didn't break your fucking nose!"

When I open the door, there sit Tom and Lance. They stand and wrap their strong young arms around me. I point to the old Ford. They nod and we all get in. The boys have packed my stuff and theirs. Nobody sings about driving on the Ghost River Road as we drive back to the tiny town with the country moon clear and bright. Lighting our way to freedom.

Kunak

KUNAK SAT ON THE SIDEWALK. HIS ASS ACHED FROM THE COLD that lay inside the concrete. A cold sensation crawled up his spine like maggots chewing their way through his body. He knew if he tried to stand, his knees would creak and crackle. Standing was getting harder these days. His brown hand flapped a Jays ball cap up and down. Panhandling was like jigging for fish. Watching the heels of the people walking past him, Kunak sang, "Come little fish, come little fish. Fill up my hat with loonies. They will make me strong. They will make me happy. Come little fish, come." The ball cap flopped up and down and from side to side in tune with Kunak's song.

Plunk! He got one!

"Ma'na ataatattiaq," Kunak whispered. He always thanked his grandfather when coins dropped into his ball cap. Once, Kunak knew Grandpa was close by him, but these days Gramps seemed far, far away. Kunak longed for him. His Gramps who gave him all he ever needed. When Kunak closed his eyes, he could see the days out on the ice with his Grandpa Chevy. Chevy would come into Kunak's bedroom early in the day and wake up him up by cupping the sides of Kunak's face into his old hands. The leathery softness of Chevy's fingertips stroked Kunak's face to the beat of his song of expectation. The song that said the fish were waiting for them.

"Irngutaq, my boy, the fish are calling our names. Irngutaq, my boy, iqaluk are singing for us. They want us to catch them and nirijuguk. They will make us strong. Open up your eyes." Kunak could see the old man hunched over his face, singing the song a little louder each time, his patience sliding away while waiting for his grandson to open his eyes.

Kunak grinned and remembered that if he hid further and further under the caribou blanket, Grandpa Chevy would soon be tickling him. It was their same pre-fishing game that they played over and over and over again. Kunak loved Grandpa Chevy more than any one person on earth.

Grandpa Chevy would say, "Oh listen, Kunak. I hear them! Listen hard and you will too! Oh, they said our names! 'Chevy and Kunak come catch us!' Get those ears of yours outta that blanket and you'll hear it too! It's such a lovely song!" Grandpa Chevy would snatch him up from under the soft fur, then tickle him until tears ran down both of their brown, chubby cheeks. It would always end with Grandpa Chevy licking his face and telling him that tears should never become dried stains. "Lick the tears on your face before they dry and nothing bad will happen to you."

Gramps and his crazy old ways. Grandpa Chevy had told Kunak many of the old beliefs but Kunak had never taken any of them inside of himself. None of the old ways had entered his muscles. None had been made room for inside his brain and heart. Even when Grandpa Chevy was alive, Kunak had refused to allow the old ways a resting place. The old ways were the old ways, he told himself. They were from times of long ago and were of no use in today's world. Let those old dogs lie is what Kunak held to be true until a coin plopped into his hat. Then he would look to the sky and whisper "ma'na" to the man who had loved him most.

Grandpa Chevy had been a wildlife guide and Kunak's only family. Chevy took the white people out to different spots on the land, showed them where to fish or hunt. He made his money that way, but Grandpa Chevy kept the true land secrets to himself. He never took the hunters and fishermen to the places of plenty. He took them to the places of moderation, to the place of Good Chances. Knowledge was something to be earned. It was not for sale and it definitely was never given away. Grandpa Chevy was a careful knowledge keeper. He made sure the customers got some of what they paid for and he was always polite. He was the most requested guide. White people loved him.

Then the Terrible Day came. The day when Kunak stood out on the porch watching for the hunters to come back in. The day that Grandpa Chevy's red toque was not in among the rest of the group. A white man came to him and said that Grandpa Chevy was lost. That they had waited overnight for him and he had not returned to their camp. A search party went out. After a week of Ski-Doos and helicopters screaming around Kunak's village, the Rangers gave up. Kunak was fourteen years old when Grandpa Chevy disappeared. He never fished again.

Kunak was alone. Times changed and no one fished anymore. Not like they used to. They ate Kraft Dinner and warmed up frozen KFC in microwaves and called that supper. The people hunted at the Northern Store. Kunak got older. He littered the tiny village with empty bottles of Southern Comfort and cheap wine. He became lost in his own little town. He didn't fit in. He was seventeen years old when he packed a duffel bag and hopped the train in Churchill.

He found day work in Winnipeg, but he wanted to be as far away from home as he could. He wanted to forget Grandpa Chevy.

He wanted to forget the old life. He wanted to forget how there were no parents to raise him. No mother to hug him. No father to call his own. No grandpa to lick his cheeks.

The village women could leave on the arms of any white man they chose. That was how they got South. That's how they got away from a life of welfare and food stamps. That's how they got out of Northern housing projects. All they had to do was spread their legs to their Great White Hope and they were headed South. Inuk men didn't have that same option. Inuk men found their Southern Comfort in other ways.

Kunak worked his way west until he found himself in Alberta. First Edmonton, then north to Fort Mac. The money was unreal. His bank account flowed over. He didn't know that so many zeros could sit in one building. On days off and back in the city he would drink and eat and fuck and sometimes he would do all three at the same time. He loved it. He loved the hard work in camp, the lifting and grunting of a labourer. He loved the exhaustion it brought and the sleep that covered him like the caribou blanket of his boyhood.

But it all dried up. He was told that oil works that way. The ebb and flow of the market. Tidal riches. After two years of no work he was sitting on the cement. His ass ached. His knees crumbled. His spirit was gone. No work. No money. No apartment. Was this Southern comfort? He spent more and more time at Hope Mission looking for anyone who looked like him. He wanted to find his own, even if it was one of those Inuk women who had fucked their way South.

There was one woman who had caught his eye. He had heard someone call her Aviak. If he got enough money from today's side-walk fishing, he would ask her to come out with him. He would take her out to Mr. Sub for a footlong. Kunak giggled quietly—he could give her a foot long all right.

The cold spring breeze made his patience slim. He checked his ball cap and saw that he had about ten dollars in loonies and toonies, a few nickels, fewer quarters. And today someone had given him a token from a casino. He placed the token into the palm of his hand, blew on it carefully and rubbed it gently across the knee of his blue jeans. When he looked at it, he saw the image of his Grandpa Chevy.

"Ha!" he shouted out loud. "I'm too hungover to think or see straight! Grandpa Chevy—as if you could sit inside a casino token!" Kunak shuffled over to the icy wall behind him and shimmied his way up, curving his hips from side to side like an old bear scratching his back against some bark. He wondered if he looked like a Northern pole dancer.

He laughed to himself, remembering the day that Grandpa Chevy tried to explain polar bear mating rituals to him.

"Now, Kunak," Grandpa Chevy began after clearing the mucus out of his throat. "Aahhhmm, now Kunak, today when we are out there on the ice . . . you know that it is springtime. Well . . . we might see some bears doing some stuff." Grandpa Chevy had said those last words very fast. It sounded like "youmightseesomebearsdoingstuff" or "umitecsomearsdoingtuff" or "youmiteseebearsuff."

"Like what, Gramps?" Kunak recalled asking. The innocence of a thirteen-year-old boy. The innocence of not understanding that the opposite sex could hold his attention longer than a game of marbles. The innocence of a boy whose voice was not crackling and whose body was hairless still. The innocence of a testosterone-free life. The innocence that lies inside of each of us when we are only a child.

"Well, Kunak. It's that time of year, you know, the time of year when a momma and papa bear look for each other. To, you know . . ."

"To, you know—what?"

"To make other baby bears . . . I mean, it's not like that happens every day for bears or for most people but most people could where bears can't and . . . shit."

"Shit—what shit?"

"It's called mating. Do you know anything about that?"

"Oh, you mean fucking? I know about that."

"You know about fucking?"

"Gramps, everybody knows about fucking."

"How? How can you know that? I didn't tell you that. And I don't call it fucking—and why are we both even saying that bad word? Is that what you think it is? Fucking?"

"That's what we all call it, Gramps. The dogs around our settlement fuck every day. It's not like I've never seen that stuff before."

"Geez Louise, boy! Do you think it's fucking when a man and a woman do it? I haven't raised you in a gutter!"

"Yeah, I do. I do think it's fucking when a man and a woman do that, Gramps. What do you call it?"

It was an honest question. An honest question because in all the years that Kunak had lived with his grandpa, he had never seen his grandpa bring anyone home. He had never, ever seen Grandpa Chevy with a woman. He had never seen him even look sideways at a woman. In his imagination, he had decided that Grandpa Chevy had been castrated like those ranch cows he had seen on TV. Or maybe he was gay? You can't be castrated and gay, he thought. Or could you? He wondered if anyone could be a castrated gay Eskimo. He was about to ask when Grandpa Chevy started to speak again.

"I call it the making love dance," said Grandpa Chevy. "It is a dance. A dance of love and there's so much work that goes into that dance. There's talking and eating and laughing and walking together. There's hugging and smiling and remembering what a woman likes. What makes her happy. There's spending time together and thinking about what your life would be like without her. Would it be better or worse? It's not fucking. It just isn't." Grandpa Chevy stared straight into Kunak's eyes and said, "You should know better."

"This is what I want to know, Grandpa. This is the one thing I want to know." Kunak said. He could feel the insides of his hands turn wet. He shifted his weight from one ankle to the next. He knew this was his one chance to ask. He blurted it out: "Are you a castrated gay Eskimo?"

Grandpa Chevy exploded. He exploded everywhere in their tiny house. His laugh hit the coffeepot and the teapot and the cups that dangled off hooks in the kitchen. His laugh hit the pillows on the couch and zigzagged over the television and ran all the way down the hall and back up again. His laugh spun around him like a hurricane and made drift piles of old laughter fall off the walls and make a mountain out of old and new laughs. His body shook and swayed and shattered into bits and pieces. Their house became the shrapnel of Grandpa Chevy's big long laugh. Kunak could only stand still and wait for his words to return.

Grandpa Chevy wiped the tears from his eyes, cleared his throat and said, "I think the answer is no."

"But Gramps, you never have a woman with you. You never bring a woman home. Look at you, all old and sexy with great hair and big strong hands . . . and no one. Not. One. How do you know all that love making dance stuff when you never show it to any woman in this town ever?" He had asked a direct, clear, concise question. Grandpa Chevy had to answer that one.

"I never bring a woman here because I have my ways. What if I fall in love with someone and you do too? What if it never works out? What if we both end up with broken hearts? I'd never do that to you, Kunak. Never. No one ever comes through the door with me.

And if a heart gets broken, it's only mine and mine is old and has been crushed over and over and over again. You don't get used to it. You just get past it."

"So, you're not a castrated gay Eskimo?"

"Nope."

"You do have a love-making dance partner?"

"Yes."

"Where do you take her?"

"My old cabin on the other side of western ridge. The one we go to when we fish in summer. That one."

"Does she have a name?"

"For me to know only."

"Is she a white woman?"

"Never."

"Why not? A lot of the people here hook up with white men and women and live happily ever after."

"Kunak, there are too many questions in your small body, and I will not answer everything today. Our gear is at the front door and we're heading out. Thanks for the good laugh. Castrated gay Eskimo . . ."

Grandpa Chevy wiped his old nose with the back of his wrinkled hand. For a moment, he realized, he and Kunak had been sharing the same memory.

"That's my boy," he whispered. He could see Kunak echo his words as he rubbed himself against the wall. Chevy was standing across 101 Avenue next to the gas pumps at the Esso station. He could not believe that he had found his boy. Chevy had been hunting and tracking his boy for the last two years. He thought about how unkempt Kunak looked. He saw how long his hair had become. Tangled. Greasy. Wearing that same red plaid jacket that Chevy had given him. It was his fishing jacket.

Chevy watched Kunak struggle to stand up. Booze, he thought. Booze got him. Chevy had hoped that booze would be the one thing that the boy would never touch. They had made a deal. No booze until Kunak's twenty-first birthday. Look at him, Chevy thought. Look at what happens when I go away from him. He's twenty-two and looks like he's fifty-two. Look at what happens. Chevy watched Kunak limp along the crooked sidewalk. Chevy followed him from the opposite side of the street, watching Kunak wave his arms and speak to the maggots inside himself.

Kunak waved his arms to shoo away the thoughts inside his head. Those were not real. What was real was that he knew one thing. He knew that if he went to the fish and chips place, they would feed him. He knew that they would give him the customers' leftovers from the battered cod. He also knew that Aviak would be there. The sidewalk in front of Fisher Joe's was her territory. Street people map out their territory the way dogs piss on trees.

"Aviak! Qanuitpit?" Kunak looked at her eyes. They were crooked. Very crooked.

"Who the fuck are you?" Aviak slurred her words. She held a mickey of Southern Comfort in her left hand. Her eyes tried to focus. She was working them so hard that you could see them grow big and small again. She was trying to find a place to put them but couldn't.

"Aviak," Kunak cooed. "Aviak, my nuliaq, I said 'qanuitpit'— how are you?"

"Huh, your wife? Fuck you!" Aviak hollered. "Fuck you and everyone like you!"

Aviak placed her index and middle fingers on the sides of her lips and let loose a long, screeching whistle.

"Trying to call the cops, are ya? We both know they don't come running for our kind. Here, let me have a seat," said Kunak as he settled down on the blanket that Aviak had spread out in front of her. On the blanket she had small drawings and rock carvings that she had made. She panhandled her artwork.

If that didn't work, she panhandled her mouth, and her crotch, and any part of her that anyone wanted. She didn't charge as much as the other women did. Not for her artwork and definitely not for her body parts that any man wanted to enjoy.

Kunak reached over and took her right hand in his. "Aviak, my nuliaq, let's find someplace quiet to go to. Someplace where we can lay in the sunshine and get some rest, okay?"

Aviak, looked at him with distrust. How many times had men said to her that they were just going to "rest?" Her long black hair fluttered into her eyes and she reached up and pulled it back too hard. When she did that, her mouth gaped open like a horse's.

Kunak could see her teeth. They were the colour of rotten apples, all brown and gooey. He shook his head and then remembered that his life was no more than what hers was. He ran his tongue around the inside of his teeth. He couldn't remember the last time he had gone to a dentist.

"Come on my nuliaq, come with me." Kunak reached under both her arms and pulled her up. Aviak reassembled herself like a wooden puppet, her dangling arms and legs falling into place as she tried to stand up straight. Her hazy head saw the black shadow. That shadow had been spinning around her all day like some pesky mosquito. Ah, must be the booze, she thought. Too much of the SoCo before sunrise. The shadow started to spin toward her. Aviak raised her hands into the air and swiped hard. "Get outta here!" she screamed, her arms flapping recklessly. "Get out! Out! Out! Out!" She looked over at Kunak.

"Bring my stuff!" she commanded. "Bring my stuff and let's go find some sunshine!" Aviak tried to smile the smile of those who are drunk. The drunken half-in-control smile that can't stay put on anyone's face after drinking. The one that lands and jumps off a person's chin like a diver. The one that can't stay put because there is really not one thing to be happy about.

"God, I hate it when those damn things show up!" Aviak bellowed. "Get outta here!" she screamed one more time. "Don't you just hate it when the bad spirits come along and get in the way?" she asked Kunak. "They're just bothersome sometimes."

Kunak grinned and wrapped his arms around her shoulders to steady her. "Aviak, we'll just go for a small walk and get some rest."

Aviak shrugged his hand off her shoulder. "Don't you talk down your nose to me, buddy! You're one of my own! You know what I'm talking about."

"Calm down, woman," Kunak said gently. "Here now. Just settle down for a bit. See, we're gonna take a small walk." Aviak stopped and stood as straight as she could.

"Can't you see her? That dark shadowy thing that keeps following me? Can't you see her?" Aviak was pleading. Pleading for someone else to see what she could see. Pleading for Kunak to tell her he could see it too. If he could, then she wasn't crazy.

"Aviak, don't worry. Let's get walking along."

"Tell me yes! Tell me yeeeeessssss!" Aviak screamed like a woman in labour. Kunak gave in. He sighed and squatted down to Aviak's eye level. "YES!" he screamed back.

"Good! There. Now we're even. Even Steven. Your name is Steven." She poked Kunak in the chest.

Kunak leaned down and grabbed the blanket by the edges. All the carvings and drawings slid into the middle. He held Aviak up as she moved her legs like Pinocchio, her knees bouncing off one another as they crossed 101 Ave and made their way to the tiny park hidden behind the pine trees.

Kunak leaned down and kissed the top of Aviak's oily forehead. "My sweet one," he whispered, "I will take care of you."

"But don't you hate it when they just keep bugging you? You know, the Evil Ones. The way they whisper inside your ears all night and tell you that you must do bad things. The way they talk to each other across the sky. The way they bug and bug and bug you until finally you just give in and say, 'Yeah. Go ahead. Do it!' Doesn't that just drive you?"

"You're talkin' old time, woman, old time. Don't even start up that stuff with me," Kunak said as he held Aviak close to his right side. He took the bottle of Southern Comfort and held it up high. "This stuff here is your Evil One and the one who talks inside your ears!"

"Listen, Steven."

"Name's Kunak."

"Oh. Listen, Kunak. I see you still got the old name. Then you understand what I'm talking about." Aviak had steadied herself enough now to stroll next to him.

"Let's just keep walking, nuliaq."

Kunak tucked the mickey into his back pocket. He could feel the small weight of Aviak leaning onto his shoulder. She must be passing out, he thought.

As they were nearing the park, Kunak was certain he could smell Grandpa Chevy. He looked in every direction. He tucked Aviak in next to him like a tiny rifle and turned to all four cardinal points to check if he could see anything. East. North. West. South. He was a well-trained guard, sniffing into the air like an old polar bear, his nostrils twisting right and left.

"Where are you?" he whispered. He could only see and hear and smell the hum of Edmonton. Inside of him was that sense of something familiar, yet out of place. The feeling you get when you long for someone or someplace or something that you know isn't near.

It was the feeling of comfort. A need for security. The yearning for home.

Grandpa Chevy stood in the middle of the sidewalk in front of the park. He heard the whisperings of Kunak as he and Aviak stumbled through his body. They did not see him, but Grandpa Chevy knew that Kunak had felt him. When Kunak walked through Grandpa Chevy's chest, Grandpa Chevy had given off the odour of home. The smell of their tiny house in the North. The smell of crisp orderliness and clean living. The smell that Kunak was raised with. The smell of harmony.

"Smell triggers memory," Grandpa Chevy thought out loud. He had seen the look in Kunak's eyes when he had the whiff of his youth reach into his brain and tap on it.

Grandpa Chevy whispered into the wind, "Kunak, my son, I will take care of you."

Kunak shivered, despite the warmth of the sun, and moved on. He let Aviak sleep off her drunkenness while he thought about Grandpa Chevy. When Aviak woke up, she reached for her notepad.

"What do you think of the evil spirits?" she asked as she started to draw.

Kunak gave her a blank look. "What evil spirits?" Kunak was thinking that Aviak was still a little drunk. Maybe she was still a little high. Maybe she was just as fucked up as he was, but in a different way.

"Didn't your Pops tell you about them?" Aviak looked him straight in the eye. Her eyes weren't rolling around in the back of her head anymore. Her black, slanted eyes were serious.

"No, we didn't talk about that old shit at home." Kunak felt uncomfortable. He could feel his knees aching.

The sun had managed to hit his shoulders between the tall pines, and it soothed his aching bones. He was in a calm place after their nap together. They had spooned like two old lovers, their shadows lying next to each other in peace.

According to the sun it was mid-afternoon, and Kunak felt full and lazy. It was quiet in the park. No one had given them any trouble for being a pair of passed-out drunks. No one had shouted the all-too-familiar words:

Move On!

Fuck Off!

You Fucking Scum!

Get a Fucking Job!

Those were the responses that street people got from the Real People. The Real People who got out of a bed each day. The Real People who went to work at a Real Job in the Real World. What dumb fucks they were.

What Kunak wanted was to stay in this place of peace and rest, without thinking about his next meal or drink or hookup. He just wanted to be still and not think about what would be next, but here she was talking about evil spirits. When the hell were his people going to let that old shit go?

"They're everywhere, you know. The Evil Ones. They watch us and at night they whisper to us and each other across the sky. They are the ones that put us on the streets. It's them." Aviak was determined to make her point.

How could she ruin such a beautiful afternoon? Kunak thought as he responded. "Aviak, if you want to believe that shit, go right ahead, and by the way, there was a guy named Pontius Pilate who really fucked things up too, but we don't talk about him 'whispering across the sky.'" Kunak made mocking quotation marks with both of his hands as he spoke.

Aviak stood up. She looked down at Kunak with complete disgust written across her mouth.

"How dare you bring the Bible guy into this! I can't stand you! I don't even know how we ended up here and together and spooning on my blanket! Get out! Get away from me! If you don't, I'll ask them to take you too! I've done it before, and I'll do it again!"

"What in hell are you talking about?" Kunak asked. "You make it sound like you're some sort of shaman or shay-woman! Like what the hell?"

Aviak lowered her voice in a very controlled manner and said slowly and deliberately, "You don't get who I am, do you? You don't get what kind of power I have. Shame on you. You with all your new Southern ways! You decided to give in and give away all that your Gramps taught you. Now listen and listen good and hard because I can get rid of you like this!" She snapped her fingers. The click sounded like the hammer on a gun. "Yes, the spirits bug me, but I do some work for them. All I have to do is whistle her in and she'll take you out. She'll feed on your soul, like a starved wolf on a caribou. They—those Bible people—used to think that we were those kinds of people. Cannon balls."

Kunak took a step back from her. "How do you know I had a grandfather?" he asked in surprise. He hadn't told her about Grandpa Chevy. "And what in holy fuck are cannon balls?"

"You went to the school in the North. Remember they taught us how those white sailors with that Franklin guy said that we ate them up? Cannon balls, asshole."

Kunak's face lit up. "Ah, cann-i-bals! Fuck, you're a piece of work, Aviak. Pretending like you're some real voodoo gitchy mama shay-woman . . . as if!" Kunak started to do the one thing he shouldn't have done. He started to laugh.

Aviak thrust her pencil at him as if it were a knife. Kunak bounced his head back from the pointed stick. He managed to stand on his creaking knees. He grabbed her wrist and twisted the sagging skin enough to make her feel a rope burn sensation.

"Ouch, you fucker!" Aviak dove at him headfirst. For an Inuk woman who was only a hundred pounds in total, she managed to generate a real force. Kunak fell back against the trunk of the nearest pine tree after hearing the empty thud of her head hitting his stomach.

"Well, you useless little cunt! You've got some fight in ya, don't you!" Kunak grabbed Aviak by her shoulders and smashed her lips onto his. He held her there until he felt the fight from inside of her start to leave. He pulled her face back a few inches from his own and said, "Now, my nuliaq, that's no way to treat your man."

"And that's no way to treat your wife, mister! Calling me the c-word! Fuck you!" Aviak tried to wrestle her way out of Kunak's strong arms. She wiggled right and jiggled left, wiggled left and jiggled right. She was trapped and she knew it. She stopped. She sighed. She let go of all the air inside her lungs.

"I just can't," Aviak said. "I just can't fight anymore." She laid her head on Kunak's shoulder and asked, "Do you think you could love me?"

Kunak cleared his throat, "How do you mean that? You know, how do you mean 'love?'"

Aviak moved her face in front of his. "I mean totally. Like how I am right now. I'm a drunk. I take all kinds of drugs and get strung out. I never know what time it is. I never know what day it is. I never know where I'm going to sleep at night. I sell my art and if that doesn't work . . . I sell me. Just so you know, all those guys whose cocks I suck or fuck, they don't mean one thing to me. Can you love that? Can you love someone like me? Could you?" Her eyes danced. Kunak knew she had said all this before to someone else. She was rehearsed. In her own awkward way, Aviak was poised.

He looked at her greasy, stringy hair and her brown teeth. Her breath smelled like a dumpster. The rest of her smelled worse. He laughed again.

Aviak snapped. She looked over Kunak's strong shoulder and nodded at the shadow that was hovering there. Ubluriaq nodded back.

A little way off to the side, Grandpa Chevy stood in the shade of one of the tall pines. He saw Ubluriaq closing in on Kunak. Chevy shook his head hard.

"That boy didn't learn one damn thing from me," he said to Ubluriaq. "Giving himself over to trash when he's already trash himself. What in hell do I do with that?"

Ubluriaq looked over at Chevy. "He's mine now. Aviak just gave him to me. I'll take him out when I please. You, you can go back to wandering around the tundra, Old Man. You won't need to follow him around anymore."

"Don't," Chevy said. "Just don't. Give him a chance. Take Aviak. She's the one that has to go. Please. And for the record, she didn't whistle."

"She did earlier in the day. She called me in like she always does. I've been waiting around for her final go-ahead. You're so busy looking in pity at your boy you didn't even notice me. He's going to be a fine meal."

"No, please don't."

"You can never call back a hit once it's been whistled in, Old Man. You already know that. See you down by the riverside. I'll be preparing supper for two."

Ubluriaq disappeared. Kunak felt a small splash of wind against his face as he wandered from the safety of the tiny park and started to walk toward 106 Avenue. This was a different area of town for both of them. Aviak's blanket was flung over Kunak's left shoulder and all her trinkets and pencils were touching one another and creating a hollow song of their own.

"Evil spirits who talk across the sky . . . where did you hear that one?" Kunak asked Aviak.

Aviak was swinging her tiny feet along on the sidewalk in rhythm with the trinkets. "My anaanatsiaq told me about them. She used to hear them at night. Especially through early winter when the sky starts to crackle with the lights. One night she took me outside and made me listen to them and I heard what they said. They told me then that I would end up South and selling myself and everything else I could. I knew I would be this."

"We should find a shopping cart," said Kunak. "A shopping cart to put your stuff in. It's easier, you know."

"And they told me that I would have a man come to me and try to make me better. Are you him?" Aviak stopped shuffling. Kunak kept walking.

"Are you him?" Aviak shouted. "Are you?"

Kunak stopped and glanced back. "Nope. Not me. Were you married to a white guy?"

"Why do you change the subject? And yeah, I was married to this guy from Norway or some place like that. I was young. Can we stop and rest?"

They stopped in a school field. There were children running around. Laughing. Playing. The way that only children do.

"Do you miss being a kid?" Aviak asked him.

"I really miss being a kid," Kunak said quietly. "I miss not having to think about my next meal. I miss being able to have my biggest worry be whether or not I was going to go fishing. I miss my Grandpa Chevy."

Aviak lay down on the cool grass and tucked her trinket blanket under her head.

"You Chevy Bass's grandkid? I knew about that guy."

"Yep. Chevy Bass was my grandpa. I'll always miss him."

"I heard he got killed by that group of white hunters. Was that true?"

"I heard so many stories about that time he took that one bunch of white guys out. No one ever knew what happened to him. Never found his body. Never found a piece of his clothes. Never found any blood or any trace of him. It was like he just disappeared. It was like he just walked away from me."

"My old gran said it was the Evil Ones. A guy like him doesn't just disappear on the land that he knows better than his own face. She said they got him and got him good. What they do to you when they're hungry is really pretty awful."

"Can you just stop with that shit? Just stop."

Kunak lay back down beside Aviak and closed his eyes. The sound of the kids playing in the schoolyard made his body relax. The sound of children can do that.

"What happened to you after all that stuff?"

"I left town and went south and then west and then north. Used to make a pile of money, but that all dried up. Now I do this. I beg on the street corners of Edmonton. I try to never stay in the same place for too long. Cops will come after you if you do."

"Those fuckers come after us no matter what. Where's the bottle of SoCo?"

Kunak reached into his back pocket and handed Aviak the mickey. She took a long swig and passed it over to him.

"No thanks. Not right now for me." Kunak handed the bottle back to Aviak.

"More for me, the merrier I'll be!" Aviak burst into a laugh. Kunak giggled with her.

"Come on, woman. We better head down the hill. There's a shortcut through the golf course close to the river and then we can cross the blue bridge and be in time for dinner at The Hope."

The Hope—what hope? Grandpa Chevy was sitting in the middle of the school field listening to their conversation. Neither of them could stick to the same subject for more than two sentences. That's what happens when booze gets you, Grandpa thought.

He stood up when they did. How do I get Kunak away from that waste of humanity? he wondered. Chevy didn't like to call favours in from the other spirits, but there came a time when you had to rely on others to get the work done. Chevy placed his tongue between his front teeth and let loose a sharp whistle.

Ubluriaq stood before Chevy. She smiled an inviting smile and whispered, "Yes?"

Chevy smiled back. "What will it take? My boy won't take the hit. He just won't. You do one thing to him. Just one push. One kick and I'll be the one you'll have to wrestle with. Me." Chevy pointed to his wide chest. "And you have to remember one thing. There's others like you that I can call in. Others who are stronger. Smarter. Like that dumb bitch said—that useless piece of scum walking next to him right now. 'You don't know who you're dealing with.'"

Ubluriaq's nose was touching his. "I'm supposed to be scared, am I, Old Man? I'm supposed to quiver and shake because of your misinformed threat. A call-in is a call-in. No take backs. No do-overs. It's on, Old Man, and I won't mind having you for an appetizer."

They watched the Inuit couple make their way along the road.

"Let's stop at the liquor store," Aviak said. Her edge was wearing off. The thing about walking and drinking is that you make the alcohol circulate faster and that hampers the enjoyment of it all. Aviak had a whisper of sweat sitting on her upper lip. "Come on! Let's stop at the liquor store!"

Kunak looked back at her and shook his head. "Nauk." Maybe he could take care of Aviak. Treat her good. Keep her sober. Live the good man's life. He wanted to get her to The Hope. Get a sandwich or something into her gut.

"No, nuliaq. Straight to The Hope for some eats." Kunak kept walking. He knew how he was with booze. He knew how it ate him up and spit him out every day of his life.

"I got money and we have to walk all the way down that big hill and then up the other side. There are some things that I don't want to remember!" Aviak pulled open the door of the liquor store on 106 Avenue. A cowbell clanged against the glass door, making Kunak stop and look back. That sound, he thought, I know that sound. I dream that sound. Except it's not a dream. It's a nightmare. That's the sound at the end of my nightmare. In the nightmare I am walking on a street at nighttime. All the city lights are off. I'm in a city of darkness and the hollow sound of a bell rings out into the night. It's the only sound there is in the city of darkness. People have turned on their car lights so they can see. In the dream, the cars can't move and the sound of the cowbell bongs over everything. It keeps ringing out over the river, over and over.

Kunak shrugged his shoulders and muttered, "Who the fuck knows. I'll wait here for a bit and see if Aviak comes along." He squatted on the sidewalk while the traffic zipped past him. Big trucks. Loud mufflers. People racing toward the river valley in a rush. High school–aged teens trying to cross the street. It was getting later in the day. School was out.

"Hey Fuck Face, where's your Walmart cart?" a tall blond boy in a basketball jersey yelled at him.

Kunak raised his hand and gave him the peace sign.

"Fuck you! You homeless ass wipe!" the blond boy strutted away.

"Here, mister," said a beautiful Black girl as she threw a toonie on the sidewalk in front of him.

"Ma'na," Kunak called after her as he made the peace sign for the second time. He looked up and smiled at the sky. "Ma'na to you too, Gramps."

A steady stream of loonies and toonies started to fall close to him. Kunak grinned. His gramps was really smiling down on him today. "Always looking after me, Grandpa Chevy."

There's an entire market at this end of the 'burbs, he thought. He grabbed the coins with his brown hand and stood to shake it all into his right pocket.

Sweet holy geez-zus! I should be here every day when school lets out, thought Kunak. He could see Aviak at the other end of the block. She was getting money put into her palm. She was smiling and, for some reason he could not understand, doing a curtsey after each shiny circle was placed into her hand.

Don't even need to say "spare change" in these parts, thought Kunak. What a haul. Such easy work. Definitely a place to return to. Let's see . . . He looked at the street signs: 106 Avenue and 82nd Street. That's the best place to stand or sit between three and four in the afternoon. Weekdays only. No Blue Jay cap jigging. Just sit and make the peace sign. Kunak began to hum as he walked toward Aviak.

"Nuliaq! Nice work. How much?" Kunak nodded toward her bra. Aviak winked and said that she had one five-dollar bill and nothing less than six toonies tucked away in her 34C cup.

"How about you?" Aviak asked, looking at his crotch.

"No money in there, babe. Got it all in my right pocket." Kunak patted his thigh and the heavy jingle of a day's work came out of the denim.

"Hey, we should be here every day, eh!" Aviak was excited. She reached into her little bundle of trinkets and brought out a piss-yellow bottle of Ungava gin. "Cool, eh! It was on sale in that cowbell liquor store! Let's sit by the river and have a sip."

"Aviak. No. We are going to The Hope to get something to eat. Half the day is gone, and we haven't even gotten down the hill. Come on. Let's just keep going. We'll be there in time for supper."

"Look at the bottle, Kunak. See: 'Ungava.' My home. Let's sit by the river and drink to my family."

Kunak gave in. "Okay. Let's go through the bush over this way." He held tight to Aviak's left arm. Women, he thought, they always get what they want.

"They do always get what they want," Chevy said to Kunak, even though he wasn't listening, "and sometimes what they don't want." He turned to the person on the other side of him. "Right, Ubluriaq?"

Ubluriaq nodded and smiled. "He's making this far too easy for me. This one will be a cake walk, or in their case, a River Walk. So simple."

Chevy felt a shiver run up his right arm and into his heart. He felt the cold splash of ice spread across his chest. Once you call any of the Evil Ones, there is no turning back. He knew that what he had asked for was the only way to get Kunak home. The only way to stop all the nonsense Kunak was living. He was doing this for his boy.

Kunak and Aviak settled themselves at a place on the river's edge.

"You know, he may have been my gramps, but I knew I was his boy," Kunak said and sucked back on the mickey. "You just know when someone really loves you." Kunak handed the bottle back to Aviak.

"Hey, take one of these," Aviak showed him a dark blue pill. "That blond boy gave me two and I already swallowed one back. Here, pop it in your mouth and take a swig."

"I'm not taking any of that shit. Never touch drugs. Never will."

"It's not like it's Viagra, you dumb fuck. Come on. The boy called it 'jackpot' and said that if I took it, I'd hit it! Come on now, let's have some real fun! Let's hit a jackpot together. Whew! That jackpot is strong. Gettin' to me already."

"Aviak, no. I mean it, no is no."

Aviak thought that the river was swaying too much. "Hey, you know what?" she said. "I had a boy. A real baby boy. He died though." Aviak's head started to sway with the river. It was the only way she could keep it in focus.

"A boy? What was his name?" Kunak stretched out his aching knees. His legs were sprawled close to the river's edge. He was enjoying the fresh smell of buds on the trees along the river. They had found a quiet spot under the blue bridge and the sounds of the city were far off. They had found their own little sanctuary. Kunak was happy here.

Aviak reached into her blanket of trinkets and pulled out a pack of smokes. She lit one and sputtered under her breath, "Called him Thomas—you know, like the apostle who became a saint of Aquino or some place."

"Oh yeah, that guy!" Kunak burst out laughing. "Tommy Aquinas! Sounds like a hardcore Eskimo to me!"

"Stop it, you dumb fucker! He was my boy. Loved him more than myself. When he died . . . I just took to the street and got away from that Norwegian and all his lutefisk. Boy, some people really know how to fuck up a good fish."

Kunak laughed at her joke. This time, Aviak laughed with him. They were both laughing. They held on to each other, laughing and rolling. Rolling and laughing along the riverbank, the water's edge coming closer to them. Kunak closed his eyes and let himself feel the moment. Ubluriaq stepped between the two rolling humans. She put her kamik under Aviak's chin and reached over to push Kunak into the river. He let go of Aviak and rolled onto his back, exhausted by the drink and the laughter.

"One swift kick," Ubluriaq whispered menacingly. "That's all it will take."

"You're right, one kick," said Chevy. Before the words could sink into Ubluriaq's head, Chevy kicked the foot that was under Aviak's open jaw. Ubluriaq watched Aviak's neck dangle to one side. Chevy put his foot under Aviak's shoulder and rolled her face first into the North Saskatchewan.

"I told you not to mess with me. I gave you the chance to do business properly with me. They say it only takes three seconds to drown," he said to Ubluriaq as he pushed down on Aviak's head. "I've called in a few of my boys, Ubluriaq. If I was you, I'd be getting outta here as fast as possible. You've fucked up and now you'll have to explain your story to them. I wonder if they'd even begin to believe you? None of this had to happen."

Chevy let go of Aviak's head. He and Ubluriaq looked down into the water and watched Aviak's body dance its final tremor before sinking to the river's muddy bottom.

Kunak opened his eyes. Aviak was gone, yet it felt like he had someone next to him. A friend. As he sat there, he realized that he did not miss Aviak.

"I know it is your doing, Grandpa Chevy," he said to the person he could feel beside him. "I'm off to The Hope now." Kunak got up and walked across Dawson Bridge, singing loudly, "Come little fish, come!"

Eskimo Heaven

I DON'T KNOW WHY I REACHED OUT THE WAY I DID. I JUST DID IT. Touched old Ittura's fingertips and we landed in a city. The tips of my fingers only brushed up against the old man's hand, and now here we are, Ittura and me. But the day had started like every other Sunday. I was preaching the early morning mass.

"Praise God!" I thundered at the congregation. "Praise God!"

The congregation stared back at me, the same stare, the same Sunday morning blank looks I got every week. Empty eyes with vacant souls. In the periphery of my vision, I imagined seeing an old Inuk in his atigi shouting, "Yes sir, Priest Prentice! Praise God!"

The congregation broke into giggles hidden behind their tanned hands, and their slanted eyes darted out from beneath coarse black bangs. I looked around but couldn't find the voice of that old man who had put a stop to the one thing I tried to achieve every Sunday—The Pure Moment.

Searching through the small group, I couldn't find the face that belonged to the voice, but instead I saw a soft glow with a black dot hovering in the cobwebbed corner toward the Gospel side of the log church. I didn't want to lose momentum and shouted one more time, "Praise God!" And again, a male voice echoed through the church, "Yes sir, Priest Prentice! Praise God!"

I was certain that the black dot had spoken. I shook my head. More giggles tucked behind brown palms, more looking to the floor. Without thinking, I shook my head to clear my mind. Shaking my head was my signal for the fiddlers and one drummer to begin the final hymn. They responded. As the music began, the black dot surrounded by soft sunlight began to float toward the back door.

The church musicians were off-key and out of time, as usual, but happily began to play, realizing that I had stopped the mass earlier than usual. Slowly, the jumble of sounds fell in together and formed a song. Little Susie Nunata broke in with the familiar words of "Amazing Grace." Her stilted soprano brought the church to life. The notes bounced off the pews and the stained glass images of lambs playing among the little lilies scattered in fields. But I barely heard the song. I was watching the black dot fade into the heavy church door.

I almost had them this morning, if only that black dot hadn't shouted out. I could have had them feel The Pure Moment—that one special time when their souls would lift from their bodies and float above the altar, higher and higher until they reached the ceiling. I knew I could have achieved that rare feat. The Holy Spirit had been so close until the black dot spoke.

How often have I preached about the goodness of life and the Holy Spirit, knowing my words were falling on the deaf ears of these Northern people. All these hundreds of years of mission work up here and they still didn't get it—but today, today they could have. Maybe, just maybe today it could have stuck better than their suicide plans and booze and the OxyContin drugs that came into town with the construction crews.

I looked out over my brown flock and smiled. Then I bowed my head and spoke softly into the only microphone in the log cabin church: "Now, tutsiavigvaa. Let us pray." I took a deep breath, looked toward the back door to double-check on the whereabouts of the black dot and began, "Lord Jesus, please bless our group of believers today and protect their hearts and souls and spirits as we each begin a new week. Bless all those that they love too and help us each to remember to keep You first in our thoughts, in our words and in our actions. In Jesus's most holy, holy name. Amen."

"Yes, sir—AMEN!" screamed the black dot in the back of the church once more. A small giggle weaved its way through the pews and some of the younger girls turned their black braided heads toward the back of the church. Susie Nunata smiled and waved to the black dot surrounded by a beautiful sunlit glow.

"What's going on here?" I asked. The congregation kept their heads down, looking intently at the wooden floor.

"What is that black dot?" No one moved. No one looked up. No one answered.

Amidst the silence, I didn't know what I felt more, anger or fear. But of one thing I was certain: whatever that dot was, I was going to catch it. I strode to the back of the church as quickly as my long legs could carry me, my eyes searching for the old black dot with a loud voice. I thought it was one of their tricks. There had to be someone who had just wandered in off the land, someone who had just come in from the spring beluga run.

The dot, the stranger with the loud voice, was no longer there. Where did he go? I stuck my head out the door quickly and scanned the flat horizon. Nothing. No one. That was weird. I shook my head again and turned back to face the congregation as they shuffled past. I shook their hands and wished them each saimmasimaniq, personal peace. It was something I truly wished for every person in the community. Peace that would keep them from reaching for the things that broke their lives and their families. I wanted that one thing more than anything for this small group of faithful and faith-filled.

When Elder Tupik came by, I took her withered hand in mine and bent low toward her near-deaf ears. "Saimmasimaniq," I shouted.

Tupik looked up at me with her wrinkled eyes and grinned. She nodded as she shuffled away. I held her elbow tightly to help her down the three wooden steps outside of the church and asked her in a low voice, "Tupik, what happened here today? What was that black dot?"

Tupik adjusted the knot of her red kerchief under her chin, looked up at me with her toothless smile and said, "Ittura!"

"Tupik, please repeat that in English," I said with a smile.

"My husband!" Tupik whispered. "He comes to church every now and again." She began to shuffle away again as two of her great-grand girls came up behind her.

"Mumiqtuq!" they giggled and scooped Tupik into their arms. They raised her small body into the air, her mukluks pointing toward the sun. Tupik burst into laughter.

"Hey, hey now," I cautioned them. "Settle down, you girls. Tupik is no spring chicken! You girls, whose voice was in church today, near the back?"

"Ataatatsiaraaluk! Our great-grandfather." The girls spoke in unison, then turned and walked away, supporting Tupik between them. I could see them whispering, heads bent to the ground.

I was confused. As far as I knew, Tupik's husband had been dead for years. These people and their belief in spirits and stupid ideas about no one ever dying unless someone is given their name. What nonsense, never letting anyone die—no wonder I had to work so hard to have The Pure Moment happen in church. No wonder I needed to say the same thing over and over again in church in the hope that just one person would begin to understand that it was time to put those old beliefs and practices away. You can't live in this century and the last century too. You must make the right choice and leave things as they are. But these people make a mish-mash of things, taking whatever suits them.

Just shake it off, I sighed. The way you shake off all the other inexplicable stuff that happens around here. Like the four-legged woman who comes out to the drum dance every year. No one ever gets in her way and they just let it go—again. At least they had all seen the black dot. At least I wasn't alone in witnessing yet another unexplained happening up here.

When the congregants had all left, I walked slowly back into the log church to blow out the candles and clean up the church. I reminded myself to make sure to lock away the communion wine. I had to padlock that stuff. How many times had the communion wine been stolen? I'd lost track. Tupik's black dot husband crossed my mind briefly at the back of the church and I decided that along with the wine, I would put away these thoughts of spirits and things that weren't real. If I indulged such thoughts, so would they. Lead by example, I reminded myself, lead by example.

I'd given the community a full decade of my life. Up here where life was very slow, and strange things happened. But today— today I had seen a glowing black dot. "Shake it off, Peter," the voice in my head kept telling me. On days like this, I miss the company of other men of faith. Men that I admire and believe in. Up here, I am alone in my faith and it is hard to keep believing that God has put me in this desert for a reason. I was making progress. Even though, like all other faiths, my church only fills up for Christmas and Easter, and sometimes the odd baptism.

Just keep believing, I tell myself every day. And then things like this happen. I touch a man's hand and look what happens! It is hard to keep on believing that it's all worth it. I have made a commitment, and even though each year I would wish that the bishop would transfer me southward, a part of me always sighs with relief when he doesn't.

Why do these things keep happening to me? I faithfully write up my quarterly reports to the diocese. There is never much change to report in them: attendance remains at a minimum, there is constant graffiti on the church exterior and the alms plate collects only the odd twenty-dollar bill. I am shepherd to a small, poor community where there always seems to be money for booze and smokes, but never enough for the collection plate.

"Just keep believing," I told myself as I tidied the church. Despite moments of doubt, I know I have been called by God to be here. I put the hymnals back into their slots. I could not help it: as I moved down the pews, I checked over my shoulder every now and again for the black dot. The quiet thud of each hymnal dropping into place in wooden pockets on the back of each pew calmed my nerves. When I dropped the last hymnal into the rack, I took the tiny key for the wine closet out of my pocket and walked up the remainder of the aisle to the altar to blow out the candles and gather the leftovers from Communion. I locked up the wine and closed the small cupboard where the communion wafers belong. I reminded myself again that God had called me here—I just needed to keep believing that.

I love the smell of old caribou hides and wax that swirl into each other inside the church. I love my weekly visits of tea and bannock with the Elders. I like going out for long walks. But mostly, I like knowing that when death visits the community, they come to my doorstep. There is a sense of security in being here. No matter how much I miss the companionship of other believers in faraway cities, I have companionship with them in spirit. When we pray, we pray as one and we feel each other's words no matter the differences that lie between us.

I hummed the ending of "Amazing Grace" as I walked back to the altar to complete my final task for the day at church. It's a habit now, something I do alone at the end of every mass. I bend my knees and pray out loud, "Heavenly Father, thank you for today."

As I said those words, the words I say in solitude every Sunday, a voice behind me bellowed, "Yeah, thank God!"

I jerked my head narrowing my eyes into each of the four corners. I could not see anyone.

"Who's here?" I shouted. Only my own voice echoed through the silence.

"I said, who's here?" Nothing again. I stayed on my knees and began to wonder about cabin fever. I know this is something that could happen to me up here. Maybe it hits you after a decade, I thought.

I shrugged and started my final prayers again. "Thank you, God, for today," I began. I paused, waiting for the interruption. Nothing. I cleared my throat, shook my head and picked up my prayer. "Thank you for all those who came out today to hear your word."

"Yeah, thanks for that!"

I sprang onto my feet and stared out at the few empty benches. "Where are you?" I shouted. My words fell into the emptiness of the church—not one sound, no visible movement, not one single body to be seen. My heart quickened a little. I pulled my shoulders back and decided to give up on prayers for the day. The church, my most comfortable place in the community, no longer felt comfortable.

I pulled my down-filled jacket on and headed toward the door. Glancing into the shadowed corners, I saw a figure of a man. An old Inuk with a happy grin.

"Who are you?" I said, hoping that the fear living inside me would not be audible. Hoping my heartbeat could not be heard. Hoping that God would swoop down from the Heavens and take me away from this madness.

"Tupik told you who I am," came the reply.

I stepped closer to the corner. I could see that the old man was fearless, that his eyes had the look that death brings—like the eyes of the blind.

"She said that you're her husband, the one I've never met, but I know you died over five years ago."

"That's right," came the reply. I could see his eyes, his constant grin.

"Tell me your name," I said.

"She told you already. Ittura." The grin, the eyes. I stepped closer still and put out my hand, trying hard to keep it from shaking.

"Well, Ittura, I'm happy to meet you," I quavered. "Really, I'm happy to meet you and glad you came to church today."

Ittura burst out laughing, "Ah, you white guys and your lines of bullshit. Really, you shouldn't bullshit in here." Ittura laughed again.

I smiled and shrugged. I didn't know what to say. I looked Ittura in the eyes and said, "It's true you've been showing up here on and off for the last five years?"

"Yeah, when I'm passing by, I always step in and look at Tupik. I know she'll be here, and I want to see her again, so I come here." Ittura took a baby step out of the shadows and asked, "You want to touch me and see if I'm real?"

I nodded my head cautiously and moved forward, fingers stretched out and trembling even though I told them not to. I felt the fur on the front of Ittura's jacket. "Rabbit?" I asked.

"Yep. Tupik made it for me."

"Why are you talking to me today?" I asked even though I know that when it comes to Elders, you never ask; you wait for them to speak. But today I wasn't going to follow that rule.

"You know, you're not supposed to ask questions," replied Ittura. "You know better than that, my boy."

"My boy." When they used that phrase, it sounded so affectionate. Like you're suddenly friends, or better yet, family. Those two words made me a little braver. "What do you want here today?" I asked, still mesmerized by the hollow, pupil-less eyes of the tiny man in front of me.

"I want you to come with me. I want you to see my world," replied Ittura. "I want you to, ah, as the young ones say, 'take a walk on the wild side,'" said Ittura with a low throat giggle. "Come with me, my boy. I want you to see the truth."

I could feel the sweat starting to build on the palms of my hands. I could feel my heart pounding. I didn't know what to do, so I said, "Listen, Ittura, I don't know what's happening right now, but this is what I'm going to do. I'm going to walk back to my house, and if you show up there, well, then I'll take that walk with you." I was trying to buy some time. I was hoping that it was just another one of the weird things that happen to people who live in isolation. A hallucination. God would never allow an experience like this to occur, not this thing that was happening right now. God would not be a part of it.

"'Fraid not, priest. It's now or never. That's the deal I'm giving out today. Don't be scared. You must see what we believe. You must understand that heaven isn't about peace, love, dove. Come along."

Ittura held out his weathered brown hand. "Just touch my fingertips and I'll take you somewhere you'd never dream of."

I touched his hand and here we were in the city.

It was loud. There were cars zipping past us, fire trucks screaming, police cars chasing the fire trucks. There were people from the South dressed in jeans and short dresses, and girls whose breasts bobbed past us.

"Nice," says Ittura as his head watches a budding cleavage pass by. "Very nice."

"Where are we?" I ask him. "What's the name of this place? I thought we were going to Eskimo Heaven." I couldn't understand any of it. A city with cars and people and plenty of noise. The constant, constant noise.

"That's where we're going." Ittura points to a building with golden arches beside it. "That's Eskimo Heaven, Father."

"A McDonald's! Are you out of your head? A McDonald's is Eskimo Heaven?" I'm furious. Why did I get suckered into an old man's game? "Get me out of here, Ittura. Now! Get me out of here!" I reach for his old tanned hands and grab them tight. Nothing happens. Not one thing. We are still standing in the parking lot of a McDonald's.

"Let's go have a Filet-O-Fish!" Ittura is happy. He's so excited to go through the doors. He strolls up to the counter, his ecstatic eyes slanted almost shut. I stand by the inside doors and watch. I wonder if the other people in here can see us. What do they see? We aren't real! Are we?

"I'll have four Filet-O-Fish, with two iced teas and two small fries!" Ittura booms out his order. The girl behind the cash register doesn't blink. She doesn't see him as odd. He's wearing his old caribou parka and his leggings are turned with the caribou fur on the outside. He is wearing one newer item—a pair of Adidas sneakers. Doesn't she see what a freak he is?

Ittura cups his hands around his mouth and yells at me, "Does that sound about right?" I look around the restaurant and nod. No one seems to notice us.

Ittura reaches into the hood of his caribou jacket and pulls out some money. I am standing next to him. I'm terrified, and the person who put me into a position of terror has become the only person who can help me. Ittura has become my saviour. God help me.

Ittura hands the tray to me. "Here, my boy, you carry it. You're still a pup." I can feel my heart pounding as I slide into the hard plastic seats of the booth. "Ittura, what is going on? Can people see us?"

"Of course they can, Father. Why wouldn't they be able to see you?"

"But look at how we're dressed! Don't they see us?"

"Oh, some of them do. You know, the people who understand the spirits. They see us."

"So not everyone can?" Ittura has shoved an entire Filet-O-Fish in his mouth. He nods.

"And the girl who took your order? She could see you?"

"Oh, yeah. That's Pokiak. She works here. Her mom was one of my wives."

"She's your daughter? How many wives have you had?" I can't believe this conversation is happening. Happening inside a McDonald's, with children and their moms and old white men sitting around us. I'm getting tired.

"Oh, so many of them. Some died. Some just left me. Some found better hunters than me and moved in with them. When I think about it, only Tupik stayed with me. That's why I visit her. Pokiak is not my daughter, but I've loved her like she is. I killed her real dad so I could be with her mom."

"Oh, God help us! I'm sitting in a McDonald's with a murderer! Ittura, take me home. I can't do it!"

"No, Father. Listen to me. It's simple logic. We were in a winter camp and I was single then. Pokiak's mother . . ." Ittura places his fingertips near his lips and kisses them. He flicks the air with them after his wet smooch. Spittle and fish crumbs sprinkle across the table like holy water from the aspergillum on Easter Sunday. "Magnificent. I needed a wife, so I killed her husband. What was that guy's name? . . . Let me think."

I lean in close to him and heatedly whisper, "This is not the time or place for confession, Ittura. Why are we here?"

Ittura looks at me and I see sadness pass over his face. His hollow eyes look even hollower. I turn my head away from him.

"I'm walking you on the wild side, Father. This is the beginning. Kakagun! That's it!" Ittura smacks his hands together. "His name was Kakagun!" Ittura's face brightens.

"Let me try to understand," I say. "You're a lonely wifeless hunter in need of a wife, so you kill that girl's father," I point to Pokiak, "and now all these years later you are telling me about it. Why?"

"To help you. Here, eat your Filet-O-Fish before it gets too cold. Cold grease is like whale blubber on a hot day." Ittura pushes the little cardboard packet toward me. I reach in and take a bite.

"I don't understand any of it. When are we going home?"

Ittura shakes his head. "Oh, we are on a journey, my boy. You have a great deal to learn. Now let me finish the story. I become a stepdad to Pokiak, but there is one understanding that Inuit have that you white guys don't. That, too, is simple logic."

I find myself thinking that if I indulge his stories, maybe I will get out of this McDonald's faster. Maybe I will get out of this surreal world and be able to get home quicker. "If it means getting out of here, Ittura, tell me the rest of your Pokiak story."

"Well, I had other children with her mom, you know. We had a couple of boys and one girl. Pretty children and clever. Oh, I loved those kids. They were our fun. When we come together as a man and a woman in a certain way, it's not about love. It's about companionship and, you know . . . well you won't know, but if you work at it, the sex can be great! Sex requires thought and you have to finesse your moves. Most things in life are about finesse."

"I am a priest, Ittura. Stop that kind of talk."

"Right, well, the rule and the logic are simple. I killed Pokiak's dad, so she had the right to kill me. And she did!"

I feel the Filet-O-Fish hurl out of my mouth. I watch it catapult into the yellow hair of the woman sitting behind Ittura. She jumps up and spins toward me. "What the fuck, buddy?" she yells. I feel her hand smack hard against my right cheek.

"I'm sorry, miss. Truly, I'm sorry. I thought I was going to choke. So I . . . I'm so very sorry."

"And look at you, buddy." The woman, who must be twenty-something, flicks two of her fingers against my black collar. "A man of the cloth! Well, I got one thing to say to all of your kind— fuck you!"

"Again, I'm so sorry. Can I pay for your meal?" I don't know what to do. Panic is all over me and I can't stop myself.

"Pay? I'm not a McDonald's whore, mister!" The young lady storms away, her four-inch heels clacking against the tile floor while the beep, beep, beep of another food order sounds in the background.

"Ittura, we have to leave! We have to get out of here. Now!" I take long strides toward the door. I glance over my left shoulder and Ittura is not moving. He's sitting there with his stupid grin and empty eyes. He is shaking his head back and forth slowly. I reluctantly return to the booth.

"Ittura, please, I am pleading with you. Take. Me. Home." I'm doing my best to control my temper. I'm doing my best to pretend that all of it is somehow normal.

"This is all part of the problem," Ittura says calmly, "and why you have to take a journey with me. You just don't get it. You just don't understand how it all works."

I am now his prisoner. I am now at the mercy of a dead man's spirit inside of a McDonald's in a strange city. I have been told "F-you" and I have watched a dead guy eat a Filet-O-Fish. And to think that only an hour ago I was complaining about my tiny congregation. I wish I was back inside my log church.

Ittura looks up. "Ah, a city bus. I love public transit—don't you, Father?" Ittura gets up and goes to the shelter to wait for the approaching bus. I stand next to him and shake my head.

"Do you even know how to get on and off a bus?" I ask.

"Of course, Father. I do it all the time when I'm in town. It's cheaper than a taxi and you get to look at all the girls. And I don't have to drive. It's enjoyable. I'd like to just settle down for a bit. I think you should too. A bus ride is a healthy choice!"

The bus stops and a woman steps off. Ittura falls into a trance. His mouth falls open. His dull eyes start to light up. The woman slides past both of us, her iPhone plugged into her ears, her sunglasses reflecting what we both look like. I see that reflection and gulp in a huge bubble of air. We look homeless. God help us.

The bus driver leans toward the door and shouts, "All aboard, boys! I gotta schedule to maintain over here." Ittura steps into the bus, drops a couple of coins and a five-dollar bill into a glass container.

"We're squared up, sir!" he shouts back at the driver and chuckles.

"You boys dressed up for K-Days?" asks the driver.

"You bet we are, sir," says Ittura. "But we're headed over to Whyte Avenue first. Gonna check out the merchandise over that way. If you know what I mean." Ittura winks his right eye at the driver, who roars with laughter.

"Okay, you boys, I'll get you there in good time." The driver waits while Ittura points me to a seat. I sit next to the window. Ittura sits next to a dark-haired woman in the seat in front of mine.

What does he think he's doing? I ask myself. I look out the window and watch all the normal people. The normal people who are walking down sidewalks with grocery bags, pushing babies in strollers. The normal people who are only concerned about making their dinner tonight. If I told them what was happening right now, not one person would believe me. Not one.

The woman sitting next to Ittura raises her hand and covers her nose and mouth. I watch her trying to be discreet about it. Not only do we look homeless, we smell homeless. People from the North will always smell different than city people. It's just the way it is. It's the food we eat. We smell like land food, no matter how many Filet-O-Fish we eat.

Ittura glances over at the dark-haired woman and says, "Problem, miss?"

"No, oh no. I thought I was going to sneeze so I'm trying to not spread it around."

"Ah, don't worry about that with me," Ittura says and straightens his back against the seat. "We worry too much about that kind of stuff, don't you think?" he asks the young lady. She smiles at him. What is it with this guy? How can a dead guy publicly schmooze women? No wonder he had a billion wives. I let out a loud cough. Ittura looks over to me and makes a sour face. The youth-filled lady bursts out laughing.

"What's your name?" Ittura asks her.

"Amanda. What's yours?"

"Ittura, but most people just call me Bill." Ittura grins and she grins back at him. I feel like I'm going to vomit. What a display. What an unholy display. A ghost and a girl on a city bus and no one else seems to care. Has God completely deserted me? Abandoned me to a ghost?

"Well, Bill, my stop is coming up." Amanda reaches up and pulls the city bus string. A low bong sounds its way through the bus. I look back out the window and turn my head in time to see Ittura make sure that Amanda must press her body against his as she moves out to the aisle. I shake my head. Ittura gives me a thumbs-up sign. Amanda stops in the aisle and leans over to Ittura. She moves her lips close to his cheek and places a soft kiss on it.

"I feel like I know you, Bill. I hope we meet again," she says as she turns. Her short skirt rustles her off the bus.

Ittura motions for me to sit next to him. I move up one seat, sit down and look straight into his empty eyes. "What was all that about?" I ask him.

"You have to study me, my boy. She understands us. She says she felt like she knew me. When she gets home, she'll think about me. She'll realize that she is somehow one of us, that we connect from the past. And we do."

I say nothing. All the double-talk that I've been putting up with. I am not in the least bit interested, but Ittura presses on.

"You see and you have to understand. Only our body dies. Our spirits live on in the world until we're assigned to one of the Lands. Of course, that's after we have been aired outside for a few days— our body, that is. The body has to be in a sitting position, with the knees close to the chest. And it has to be wrapped in a good fur and leaned up against the igloo or tent, depending on the season. We need that time to sort ourselves out once we're not in body form."

"And how long does that take?" I ask dryly. My patience is wearing thin. I'm sweating on a city transit bus. Not one window is open.

"Ah, our stop is up ahead. Okay, I'm ringing the bell. My favourite part!" Ittura leans past me and pulls the string. "Let's roll, priest!"

We're walking west on Whyte Avenue. It's hot out. I wish I could take off my black jacket and my collar. I wonder if dogs ever feel that way about their collars. They must.

"Let's go in here!" Ittura is practically running down the sidewalk. He takes me past a restaurant with an outside patio and tables. He trots past a Fat Franks. He looks awful in his caribou jacket and pants. He stands next to a bar and holds the black door open for me.

I put my hands up, "Stop right there! No bar for me! I don't do that!"

Ittura bends low and says, "Step in, Father. You're about to enter the Wild Side."

"Ittura, listen, I've been tolerant over the past couple hours. But come on, a priest and a ghost walk into a bar . . . come on!"

Ittura nudges me through the door. There's air conditioning in the bar. I'm grateful for that. I take off my black jacket and slip it onto the back of my chair. Ittura stays fully dressed.

"Take off your jacket," I say. "Relax!" I've given up. I've given in. I can't fight what I can't stop. I tell myself to take deep breaths and to just enjoy the moment.

"I got no shirt on under my caribou coat," Ittura whispers into my ear. "If I take it off, it's just my hairless bare chest, and we don't want everyone to see that."

"Why not? Do ghosts have some sort of uniform protocol?" I am beginning have fun despite myself. Just go with it, I keep repeating, hoping that if I don't resist, I can be out of here sooner.

"Well, son," says Ittura, "my chest is smooth because hair can't grow on steel!" Ittura breaks into laughter. "A Native guy told me that once. Funniest thing anyone ever said to me."

I shake my head, "And when was that? After you killed his brother so you could get his wife?"

Ittura takes me seriously. I didn't mean to be misunderstood, but here we are. He leans close to me and says in a low voice, "Number One: We're not ghosts. We're anirniq—spirit. Number Two: I did what I had to at the time. Number Three: If you're gonna learn one damn thing today, it's to listen! I'm the teacher. You're the student and you can't hear nothin' when those gums keep flapping. Got it?"

"Well teach, what do you think I've learned today? I've learned that I should have never touched your hand. I learned that Eskimo Heaven is a McDonald's restaurant. I've learned that you love all women, and the younger they are, the harder you fall. I've watched you lie to a bus driver—K-Days, my foot. And now, here I am in a dirty blues bar. Let's just say your 'teaching' requires more finesse." I say all this while leaning across the table. I'm staring deep into his eyes, trying to get in his face. I'm trying to go with it all, but a part of me just can't.

Ittura takes up the challenge. He places his elbows firmly on the table and leans in toward me. With every word, his worn face gets closer to mine.

"Another one of the problems is how you white guys don't think beyond your lily-white noses! A whole lot of teaching went on so far today, but you just can't see it!"

Ittura is getting riled. For as long as I've worked with the Inuit, seeing them get angry does not happen. It's just not in them. Our nose tips are locked into a duel. Whoever pulls away first is the loser. We stay nose to nose until the server comes along.

"Hey, you guys must be going to K-Days! What would you fellas like to drink today?" Her voice breaks up our nose fight. We both pull back at the same time. It's a draw. Nobody wins.

"I'll have a ginger ale," I say, "and so will my friend." I look at Ittura in complete disdain.

"Oh, no, sweetie, no ginger ale for this old Inuk. I'll have a cherry whiskey on ice." Ittura keeps his eyes stuck on me and adds, "Make that a double!"

The music is blaring against the smoke-filled walls in the blues bar. A bald man with a harmonica is singing about how we all come from Africa. His lyrics are telling us over and over again to go back to Africa. The over-fifty crowd are attempting to gyrate their ancient hips to the rhythm of African drumbeats. I find myself thinking that there is nothing worse than watching old people trying to dance.

Ittura and I haven't spoken since the band started playing. We have maintained half an hour of silence. We have not even glanced at each another. Inuit shun you when they are angry. That much I do know.

The atmosphere is musical confusion. I don't know how much longer I can take it. Do I have to stay with Ittura? What if I just walked out of the wild side and went off on my own? What's the worst that could happen to a priest on a sunny summer afternoon? I reach behind my chair and stand up. As I'm putting on my black jacket, Ittura's chin juts out at me. Inuit speak with their eyes and chins. I know that he's silently asking me, "What are you doing?"

"I'm out! I've had enough," I scream over the music. "You can sit here all day if you like, Ittura, but I can't. See you later." Ittura makes no effort to follow me. When I glance back, I can only see his caribou hood. He doesn't give one damn about me.

The noise of the city street is soothing in comparison to the racket of the blues bar. The cars, the people, the heat. I feel free for the first time in hours. I slide my hands into my pockets and realize that I have the money from the collection plate with me. I stroll over to the hot dog place and order one fat dog with the works. I sit at the only picnic table available.

"Hey," says a male voice. I look across the table, smile and extend my hand.

"Hi, I'm Peter Prentice. Is it okay if I sit here?"

The boyish-looking man takes my hand in his and shakes it firmly. He is the first person that I've met today without Ittura. He is my second contact in the modern world. The first one had said, "Fuck you" in McDonald's. In a strange way, this guy brings me some comfort. I feel like I've found some normalcy.

"Of course. I see that you're a holy man. Catholic?" A grin emerges from behind the beard that all under-thirties wear these days.

"'Fraid so. Is that a problem? I can move."

"Nah, not a problem for me, preacher-man. What are you doing in the city? I mean, like, where do you preach?"

"Oh, I'm just in town visiting. I live way north of here. I have a small church in a little Northern village." I hear the vendor yell out my number. "I'll be right back." I go over and pay way too much for a hot dog but convince myself it's okay because it does have the works. I begin to salivate. The smell of cooked onions must be one of the best smells in the world. I carry the hot dog back to the table cradled in my hands like a newborn. I'm so very happy.

"Hey, sweetie," I hear as I'm sitting back down. The bearded boy is gone. There's a woman sitting across from me instead.

"Hey, where did the young fella go?"

"Nowhere."

"Okay," I reply. I just want one big, fat, juicy bite out of this dog. One bite without any weirdness. I have no further questions. My lips approach the hot dog, my jaws start to open and I prepare to bite down.

Just as my tongue begins to flatten, the hot dog flies from my grip and across the sidewalk. It splats like an egg in the midsummer heat. I can't believe it. I cannot believe it.

Ittura snaps his fingers around my arm. His teeth are bared, but not in a smile. His eyes are almost shut as he grabs my elbow and lifts me off the table with all his strength.

"Run! Ajujuq!" I start to run across the blues bar parking lot. It's loaded with bikers and everyone is smoking weed. I feel like my surreal world has fallen into a rabbit hole. This can't be real. All I can do is keep running. I trust that Ittura will find me.

I lean up against a fence in front of a house. This street is quiet, and the shade of the big trees covers me up in a cool blanket. I am finding my breath. I am panting so hard I feel tears start to well up in my eyes. I want to go home.

"Hi!" I glance up and there is Ittura sitting on a tree branch. His feet swinging back and forth like a child's. He starts to whistle.

"You creep! You took my hot dog away!"

"I saved your fucking life, preacher!" Ittura snarls and jumps from the branch like a cat. This guy has nine lives.

"What the heck? What was all that?"

"Must be hard to be a priest and not be able to swear. Is it hard?" Ittura asks his question in earnestness.

"You want me to swear? Okay, I will! You dumb fuck! You stole the only food I wanted to eat today!"

"I didn't steal it. I had to get your attention. You don't understand."

"I understand nothing! Nothing about this entire day! Not one silly second of it!"

"Father Peter, you were sitting with Nananuak. She is the Evil Spirit. The worst one."

"But I didn't talk to her. I didn't do one thing! I wanted to eat my hot dog!" I am whining like a four-year-old child. I don't care.

"Was there a man there before her?"

"Yes, but what does that matter?"

"Her name is Nananuak. Nananuak was a woman who went into the Land of the Dead. She just broke through without having died herself. When she was there, she changed into a man and then returned home to her husband. After that, her husband wouldn't sleep with her. Or him. Whatever. So her husband made a plan to kill Nananuak, but she got him first. She sliced his throat open and watched him bleed out. From that moment on, she became the Evilest Spirit among the spirits in the Land of the Dead. She travels across the North killing people at will. We must pray for protections from her as soon as a new baby comes into our communities or she'll slice their throats. Then she comes South and does the same. She was the lady across from you. He was the man across from you. I keep telling you that you aren't listening or learning. You have to do that, Father. You have to take the time to learn who we are. What is real to us."

Ittura sits down on the sidewalk. I sit down next to him. I look into his eyes and say, "I'm ready, Ittura. I'm ready to learn. I won't interrupt you anymore."

I'm not giving up or giving in. I am finally ready to take it and learn.

We are walking down the long, winding sidewalk. The North Saskatchewan River is waiting for us. There are people running past us in shorts. Joggers. Women pushing strollers while they run, their faces filled with perspiration. They breathe in deep breaths of hot summer air.

I look over at Ittura and say, "What do you make of these people running everywhere?"

Ittura shrugs. "It's something they like to do in the South. I have no idea what they are going to accomplish with it all. It keeps them busy down here since they don't have to worry about finding their suppers. They just go to a Safeway or some place that sells 'organic' vegetables. Do you believe that 'organic' is really organic?" This is the first time Ittura has asked for my opinion on anything.

"I think that all 'organic' means is that the food was grown in horse manure."

"I think the entire South is horse shit!" Ittura starts to laugh. I look over to him and smile.

We reach the riverbank and find a spot of shade to sit in. We don't speak. I think that we are both exhausted. I won't say anything. I've been told to listen.

"Okay." Ittura clears his throat. "Remember Pokiak—the girl at McDonald's?"

I nod. "You killed her father and then she killed you."

"That's right! Now you're being a good student. A good listener." Ittura slaps my shoulder. "Inuit are allowed to even the score that way, and there's not one thing the cops can do about it. It's our maligaq, our law."

"Can I say this, Ittura? That's not law. That's murder."

"See, that's the way everyone else thinks. For us, it's okay to take another man's wife. We just need to get that man out of the way. Simplest thing to do is to kill him!"

"That's not simple. That's complicated," I respond.

We've both stretched out in a shady spot. The river sings a soft song in the background. This is the most relaxed either of us has been today. Ittura has removed his caribou parka and leggings. He is almost naked, except for his Adidas running shoes and the white tube socks that sit below his brown kneecaps.

"That's how you guys think. It's like this. I killed Kakagun because I needed a wife, but I know one thing. Any of his children can, at any time, kill me. That's the risk I take. I become their stepdad, but Tupik would have told Pokiak that I killed her dad at some point in her life. She then has the right to kill me. To even the score that way. And I spend my life wondering when that will happen. Simple."

"And she doesn't get in any trouble with the RCMP?"

"Of course not! We don't tell those guys too much. They just interfere in our affairs. But you gotta remember this: an Inuk only tells half of the story. All those anthropologists and cops, and those people from the big Southern businesses—we don't tell them everything! We can't."

"So, how did she do it? Pokiak?"

"We were out fishing, her and me. Tupik stayed home with the others, who wanted to watch TV. So Pokiak and I were out one evening and she keeps asking to go farther out on the bay. That's when I knew it was going to happen. I flat out asked her if it was time. She nodded. When we were far away from town, she asked me to stand up. I did, and she blew my ass right out of the boat! BAM! Done!"

"And what did she say to everyone in town?"

"That I drowned, but they all knew better."

"Didn't the cops look for your body?"

"They did, but I hid from them. I went deep, onto the floor of the bay. Just stayed there for a week or so and then came back up. I'm still wandering around waiting for someone to take my name, and then I can move on to one of the Lands. In the meantime, I get to talk to you."

"You've been gone for a lot of years, Ittura. What else do you do besides bother a priest?"

"Oh, I help Tupik when I can. I make sure to bring her some fish and leave it at her door. She always blows me a kiss and says, 'Ma'na Ittura.' I still love that woman. We both know the day will come when I must move to one of the Lands. And I come down here and make sure Pokiak is okay. I leave fish at her door too. That's what us spirits do. We make sure our families are doing all right in this world. Try to help when we can. Sing songs to them when they are having bad days. Sleep next to them at night and rub their foreheads. Push cars and bad people out of their way. We just try to make sure that their lives here are as good as we can make them."

"What about Eskimo Heaven? When are you going to go there?"

Ittura breaks into the biggest laugh ever. "There is no Eskimo Heaven!" His laughter grows and grows until Ittura is rolling from side to side. He has big tears falling down his chubby face and he can't stop. I join in. He's having fun. I want to have this same fun. Somehow, we can't stop. I start rolling from side to side. I laugh until my ribs ache. We end up rolling into each other and eventually through our laughing tears manage to help each other sit up.

"Then tell me why we went to McDonald's?"

"'Cause I wanted to see Pokiak. And I really do enjoy the Filet-O-Fish!"

Our laughter has cooled to a simmer.

"What do you really believe, Ittura? Is there Heaven? Is there Hell?" I have to ask. This is maybe the only time I will get to know what they believe.

"Father Peter," Ittura looks at me. "There's only Now. That's what we believe. We don't spend Now building up merit points. We spend Now helping in the ways that we can. We are a small group. We have to send love to each other. We have to be kind to everyone.

But that isn't because we are on a points system. It's because that's how we survive. It's because that's how we make it in the Now world—not the next world. It's how we can keep our children with us. We can only send love. That's our purpose here."

"But you guys pray and sing and believe there is something bigger than you."

"We do, Father Peter. We sing to our ancestors that are with us. We thank them for staying beside us. Not one of us, including you, would still be here without them. You need to start saying your prayers to them too."

"Ittura, I went to school to learn about it all. I can't change that part of me."

"No, you can't, Father Peter. You can do one thing. You can start to think about other ways and don't think of them as wrong or less than. Just love us, Father. That's all we want. And give back to us in gentle ways. It's not about Our Fathers and Hail Marys—it's about the Now."

"I can start to do that, Ittura. I can start to try. Would that be enough?"

"Of course! Do you want to go home?" Ittura starts to put his parka and pants back on.

I reach out my fingertips to him. He reaches out his to me.

THE FOLLOWING SUNDAY I AM SMILING OUT AT MY CONGREGATION. I am back on the quiet tundra. I am home, back where I belong. We sing our jumbled out "Amazing Grace," but today it doesn't sound like a mess. It sounds like something that would play in the Vatican. It sounds beautiful.

I walk Tupik to the door of the church and hold her elbow down the stairs. She leans into my ear and says, "I hear you went to the city."

I nod and smile at her. "I learned many things that day, Tupik. Ittura was good to me."

Her face crinkles up and her toothless smile stays frozen for a moment. "He can be a bugger, that man! But he always means well. We have to see the good in everything, you know."

"I think I'm beginning to. When do you expect to see him again?"

"Oh, I don't! He's off in one of the Lands. One of my grands called her dog 'Ittura' so he's not wandering around anymore. She'll be forced to treat that dog well, but it was me, I wouldn't let him go for all these years. Wouldn't let the new ones be named after him. Selfish, eh?"

"Not at all, Tupik. Not at all. He taught me things. Things that I needed to know."

Tupik hunches over her cane and begins her long walk home. I feel a sadness come over me. No more Ittura at church. As I turn to head back up the wooden steps, I feel a soft caress across my forehead.

I stop and smile and whisper, "Ma'na anirniq."

Panem et Circenses

A QUIVER OF WOMEN. EVERY AFTERNOON FROM TWO TO SIX THEY are wine aficionados. Every now and then a man joins the group. They squirm if a man comes along. They slither and slide from side to side. Countless trips to the ladies' room. Adjust lipstick. Comb hair. Return to the table acting coy and different from one another, yet they are the same.

They want one man to look at them. They want to feel wanted. They want his attention. What they don't want is to fuck his brains out.

They want to feel as though they have him on a line that they can reel in and out. Play with him like a hooked fish. Whistle to him like a puppy. Of course, he must be eager to have their company.

They are all millionaires. Money is the cord that ties them to one another. Their common form of bondage. Their goal now that they have reached their later years is to accumulate more of it. That cannot be done without a man. A rich man. He must have more in his account than they do. He must be richer.

He doesn't need to be handsome. He doesn't need to have social grace. He doesn't need to have all his teeth in his head.

He must only be richer. His bank account must brim over and spill onto a balance sheet that is long and large. Zeros are his biggest asset.

They sit like cobras in a charmer's basket, weaving their heads at the stranger among them. Waiting for the right moment to strike. Careful. Calculated.

The man must be older. Not wiser. Older. Age is his advantage. Their cobra dance heightens as they gauge his worth. A slight slither to the right. A longer lean to the left. Hissing and sizzling like bacon coming to life in a sexy cast iron pan.

Their black mascaraed eyes are heavy with pseudo-passion. "Please look my way," they moan while they adjust their V-neck sweaters to show off their crinkled breasts.

They hope he has friends. They hope he has friends who are richer than he is. He must. He travels in the rich men's circles. Former businessmen and now property owners. These ladies had strict entrance requirements to their club. Membership tallied up to double-digits plus seven successive zeros: anything less than that amount in a man's bank account and their attitude towards zero-tolerance would appear.

The women weave their heads together, clinging to his every word. Their dance of welcoming their prey to the party. If he dares to glance at his cellphone, they hiss, "Begone! You are not paying attention to us." They require a man's full attention. No distractions. No deviations.

That is the scenario every afternoon. The Rich Widows' Club. Women who screwed their way into mansions and rich men's beds. All they ever had to do was screw. And that they did in their younger years. Now they have retired from the opening of legs and the swallowing of cum, but their bank accounts still drive them to do things that others may not. Their obsession with money didn't retire at age sixty-five. Now they have to think about what they are leaving to their grandchildren and the great-grands.

Their legacies lie in their bank accounts. Not who they are or were but what was left to them when each successive husband died off. Accountants and lawyers manage their lives. They understand what they have and how it works. They may appear to live shallow lives. On-the-surface lives that are in perfect order. All their ducks floating on the money they have never earned, lined up row after row.

Rich widowed women are not the only ones who play this game. Rich widowers play it too. It is like a bad game of Monopoly in which no one gets out of jail free. "Do not pass Go" means you must find another way to build your bank account. Building a bank account requires cunning. It requires skills that are not taught in school. It requires careful observation and knowing exactly when to strike. It requires the understanding of rules that will never be put into print. It does not require love. It does not require a kind heart.

Jared Johnson, or JJ, as he'd been called since birth, is on a hunt. Not for sex. Not for the comfort of a relationship. He needs a business transaction. He has a winter trip coming up and needs a woman at his side. Someone who is close to his age. Someone between sixty-five and seventy. Someone who knows how to play the game of the Rich Companion. A game that JJ is familiar with. A game he played often in his younger years. He knows the poise that is required.

Good posture. She needs to have it. A strong, straight back. Muscular calves. Shapely legs. No tree trunk ankles. No wide, flat ass. Firm ass. Firm tits. He doesn't care how she got them. If it means she has to wear a bedazzled double wire push-up bra or have buckets of fat liposuctioned out of her, he doesn't mind. What he needs is someone who can smile and nod. Someone who he does not need to impress. Someone that he will not want to touch. He needs a Bobblehead Widow and he knows where to find one.

JJ knows the cost of divorce. He has lost three houses and parts of his pensions to divorce, not dementia. Now, in his seventy-fifth year, he has been given the investment opportunity of his ever-shortening lifetime. His years are numbered, and he knows it. Maybe ten good ones left. Five for sure. He needs a woman who understands what he wants. She also needs to understand that he is not going to pay for the time she spends with him. He will pay the cost of travel and food.

JJ knows about the Rich Widows' Club through some of his old business acquaintances. The Rich Widows who drink daily wine and eat daily bread in upscale venues, proclaiming themselves to be foodies. They are not women who cook or clean or read a newspaper. Facebook informs their lives. All of their knowledge arrives via social media posts. He has seen some of their reactions on Facebook. Their likes and dislikes in fashion alongside of their hourly likes and dislikes of one another. He has been anonymously trolling them online. Gazing at their personal pages, hitting thumbs down on their fashion and food choices, chuckling in the afterglow of their outraged reactions at home in his office. He knows that they are women who understand the game. He knows that their leader has taken up this sort of work in the past.

Her name starts with the letter *P*. What was it again? Priscilla? Patty? He knows she is a prima donna. That starts with a *P*. He'll just think of her as Prima: Number One. The Latin sounds old and foreign and fancy, like her. He'll just name the others in sequence: Secunda, Tertia and so on, until the numbers line up nicely. Then, when he has chosen his companion, he only has to remember one name.

"Don't need to worry about banging those old gals," his buddy told him. "They will tell you straight out that they are closed for business. But they work at not looking like antiques!"

JJ trusted his friend. He has done his research. He feels confident as he strolls into the dimly lit lounge, adjusting his tie.

"*Avete mulieres!* Greetings, ladies! *Omnia pulchriora lupi sunt*— you are all as beautiful as wolves!" JJ says loudly and all too enthusiastically, showing off his schoolboy Latin. It always seemed to make an impression on the ladies. "I'm JJ, and my buddy Roy has given this group a good reference. May I join you?"

The women move their heads in closer to the man. Their richer-than-them man. JJ all-too-casually mentions his yacht and his winter trip to the Bahamas. He says he is weary of travelling alone. He would like a companion. The ladies giggle in unison. He feels confident that he has come to the right place. The Queen Cobras see a man who will pay for their time away. They would never need to touch their own precious bank accounts.

They wait for one of them to strike out. They wait for Prima, their leader with the forked tongue, to spit out the words that they all long to say. She is richest. She has earned the right to speak first.

She stands tall, like the hostess of an important event, placing a gold-plated pen in her right hand. She uses it to point as she introduces the nest of five women. They have names, but all JJ hears is Secunda, Tertia, Quarta, Quinta. They each nod in turn, running their eyes up and down JJ's well-kept frame. They are quietly assessing the cost of his suit, his shoes, the silk handkerchief in his lapel pocket. They are searching for signs of gold jewellery. Rings, bracelets, cufflinks, the make of his wristwatch. They are checking his hair. They know the difference between a barber and a stylist. They each know how a man with more money than they have should present himself. He is the Ken to their Barbie.

JJ feels all ten eyes tearing him apart. He knows what their looks mean. Rich men are not stupid. Shallow perhaps, but not stupid. If they were, they would not be sitting with all their zeros surrounding them like soft pillows. They know what women of wealth are like. They are all playing the same game, the game of obvious wealth. How do they each wear it? JJ offers to buy the next round of Happy Hour wine. Rich men know to never pay full price.

JJ is not foolish. He knows he is now the snake charmer. He knows how to reel them in and have them dangle in front of him. Their breasts swaying like the teats of a Holstein. Their dry vaginas lubed with Vaseline. He knows their tricks. He knows how far each one of them will go, in and out of bed.

JJ needs someone who will be his trophy companion. Someone who will make him appear even more respectable. Someone who can stand next to him and smile. That's all she has to do. She has to smile the smile of his success.

While they measure him, he measures them. From first glance, considering the obvious amount of eye makeup, hair dye and material of their clothing, he knows that each and every one of them is well-maintained by various vendors. Hermès, Dior, Dolce and Prada are on display in clothing and jewellery. Each of their ten hands is heavily polished with colours carefully chosen to match the shades of their dresses. Lips are laden with slices of beet-red lipstick. Their smiles are an exercise in heavy weightlifting. They are not women who smile with ease.

JJ must make it known that the woman he chooses should not speak. She is without an opinion. He knows the afternoon quiver are already skilled, well trained and experienced in what he needs.

He does not want brains, and he is confident that these old gals can learn new tricks.

After the quick introductions, Prima speaks. Her breast implants have remained firm because of all the oil she wraps them in night after night. She bats her blackened lashes and hisses that she would love to travel on a yacht to the Bahamas. She has not done it for decades. JJ smiles at her and asks the most important question: "How much is your out-of-country medical insurance?"

Illness and death factor in heavily for the aged. Moving about is no longer done freely within their own bodies or outside of their own country. Broken hips are without borders.

She stares into her glass of Judgment of Paris Chardonnay, calculating the cost. She knows instinctively that her chances are greatly reduced. She will have to use all her cunning if she is to accompany him. He will not take her cost-free unless she offers payment on the extra health coverage. Does she want to spend any of her own money on him?

JJ is now an investment. Like a stock or a share in a company. The blindfold of Lady Justice has been removed and the scales tip hard to the right. Placing one hand on the table, her index finger taps twice, the Azature polish sending sparkles into the afternoon. She has signalled the next in line to move into position. Prima is a good poker player. She passes.

JJ notes the gesture. *Illa recederit a ludo*, he thinks. She withdraws from the game. For now. Smart woman. She understands investment. She understands the importance of hanging on to her capital. He knows she won't travel with him unless she has weighed her options. He is a patient auctioneer. He awaits the next bid.

Secunda is sitting beside him. She has creamy white skin, the blonde hair of Debbie Reynolds, the red lips of Audrey Hepburn and the innocent looks of Betty White. Secunda would fit the bill. She smiles the perfect smile. Her dentures are stainless. Her weathered hands are well manicured. Secunda wiggles her chair closer to his, close enough for them to rub shoulders. He feels the heat of her and turns his eyes toward her zig-zagging head.

Secunda explains that her health is robust. Perfect. She has soldiered through the illnesses of her three dead husbands and never caught what they had! She is the epitome of well-being. JJ examines her face and sees a twitch under her Diamond's Red lipstick.

A slight imperfection. Something she appears to do unconsciously as she speaks. A miniscule pucker. Like a fish inside a glass bowl, her lips purse together at the beginning and end of each sentence. A symptom of Tourette's? *Illa est uitiosam colit:* she is flawed. He uses the last of his stuttering juvenile Latin to help him make up his mind: He cannot take her with him. He must find a way to discourage her.

"The husbands," he asks. "What happened to them?"

"Oh, crazy, unexpected things. One fell forward, the other backward and one just lost his marbles! All of them!" Secunda replies in a perfectly-puckered-start-and-finish sentence. Her smile is the end stop to her explanation.

"Fell? How? What caused the falls?"

"Slippery bathtubs and sidewalks. You know, a fall at our age is so dangerous. I installed a walk-in shower. Do you have one?"

Secunda is changing the subject. He can feel her body temperature begin to drop. He can feel the ice that surrounds her heart spreading to the tip of his shoulder. She is cold, he thinks. Icebergs have been building inside of her for years. She is dangerous.

A package of Hollywood perfection on the outside, diabolic on the inside. He wonders about the sudden falls of husbands now safely tucked away at the local cemetery.

Tertia pushes past Secunda. She literally lands in his lap. With a gush of surprise, she exclaims, "Oh, look! I fell in sideways! How silly of me! None of her husbands ever did that! Fall sideways, that is." Tertia throws back her head and laughs herself into hysterics.

"Good thing I put on Depends before I left the house!" she guffaws as she leans toward JJ with a wink, sliding her slim fingers into the crease of his crotch. He jerks back slightly and then decides to lean forward. Let her rub, he thinks. Rub-a-dub-dub all the way to the Bahamas and back.

Tertia is not like the other cobras. She doesn't have the giant head swaying from side to side. She has one thing that the other two do not. A waistline. An hourglass figure that she has kept under glass for all her decades on earth.

JJ sees her up close. Her implants are huge.

Not her breasts. Her teeth.

Giant white dental implants that blend in with her makeup. She must own stock in Estée Lauder, JJ thinks. Her foundation makeup has been put on with a roller brush dipped into a house painter's tray. The cracks and crevices of her cheeks remind him of the hoodoos in the Alberta Badlands.

"Gosh, I'm just joking about the Depends," she sighs as she struggles to move away from him. He watches her hold tight to the table edge and the back of his chair. His crotch feels the cold air of the lounge swoop in on it. He closes his legs.

"Hip problems?" he asks. Her imperfection.

Tertia grins. "Too much golf this year! I can't stop myself with that stuff!"

"There's golf in the Bahamas. Ever been to Paradise Island?" he asks. She will bite on this, a camouflaged invitation.

"Never!" exclaims Tertia. "But I have been to Gilligan's Island!" She bends forward and laughs, posing like a donkey, head pushed forward, teeth in full view. Her braying snort rattles the wine glasses on the table.

JJ swears he can hear the hee-hawing of an entire herd. *If I could be sure she would never speak*, he thinks. He watches her, squinting his eyes. *Not bad on first glance, at least compared to the others.* JJ decides to bait her a bit more.

"Gilligan's Island?" he asks, "Where is that one?"

"Poor-oit-toe Reekoo," Tertia declares, looking into his blue-sky eyes and spinning the *R*s like the wheels on a walker.

"Did you see Gilligan and the skipper too, the millionaire and his wife, a movie star and of course the professor and Mary Ann?"

JJ bursts out laughing as the cobras begin to sing the theme song from the old TV show. He has won them over. He has stirred a happy memory in all of them. He orders a third round for the table, while measuring their response to a show about a group of castaways stranded together on a deserted island. They are self-made castaways. A posse of pariahs.

JJ slips his thumb and forefinger into his barely opened Joy-nin handstitched leather wallet. He makes sure the women have enough time to recognize the brand name and quality before he slides out his black American Express Centurion credit card. He holds it close to the table, making sure it faces the snake pit. He sees their smiles. He is pleased to see their silent acknowledgement of his piece of plastic. He knows his significance score has gone up a notch.

"I've always wanted one of those," says Tertia mournfully. "My ex almost got one but when he was refused—believe me, that was Game Over!" she brays quietly.

"I have one," says a sultry voice. JJ looks to the opposite side of the table and sees Quarta dig into her Hermès Birkin bag. She holds her card over the tabletop, mocking JJ.

Quarta is not a white woman. She appears to be Native. Native from where is what JJ wants to ask, but he doesn't know how or when to say the words. His profession as a lawyer has taught him to never solicit information directly. JJ muses about how odd it is for him to see the black card coddled in brown hands. Chubby, round brown hands but hands that appear strong. His imagination momentarily floats into a tipi.

JJ takes a swig of his Pappy Van Winkle bourbon. He grins and looks longingly at her full, toast-coloured breasts.

Quarta squishes her credit card into her cleavage. The sound of silicone sloshing is almost audible. The perfect frame for such an exclusive card. Her middle finger covers the imprinted name, making Prima lean in closer. "Is that really yours?" she demands. "Show me the name on that card!"

Reluctantly, Quarta removes her finger and slides the precious piece of platinum toward her leader.

"There. You called me out. It really belongs to my son," she says. "I asked him if I could bring it today for show and tell."

The group giggles, but it sounds more like hissing. Steam escaping under pressure. Stress release. Quarta, they already know, is far from being above any of them. After all, she rents her condo. She was allowed into the group as a reminder of what they each once were. Poor and alone. Someone who sat on the outside of life. Someone who was picked last for everything in school, and even though Quarta married well, her skin colour keeps her on the edge of the circle.

Quarta knows that, but it doesn't bother her. Not anymore. It is what she lives every day of her life. Her skin sets her aside. Makes her different. It bothers them and that's all that matters to her.

Honesty in this one, JJ thinks. That can be a good quality in a companion. Simpleness too. Her eyes and lips are pretty much painted on and she has the chubbiness of a matronly woman. Someone who would not draw attention to herself in a room. Her skin colour could pass as a suntan.

"How many children do you have?" he asks her.

"Just my one boy. Well, he is a full-grown man now. I miss him," sighs Quarta. "I miss him being a little boy. You know, the fun it all was when he was small."

JJ nods and studies Quarta a little more. She holds the most promise. Her sexy voice. Her honesty. This afternoon is better than online dating. Easier. Instead of one at a time, JJ has his pick of five live women and number four appears willing and definitely able. JJ is loving this version of *The Dating Game*, where he is able to see their faces and body shapes.

"Any grands?" JJ pursues his interview.

"Not one," purrs Quarta. She recognizes that his attention has stayed with her longer than with the others. Her slanted brown eyes stay fixed on his. The other cobras observe the non-verbal contact. They know that mesmerizing a man is the most important part of the catch. If they cannot get a man with their boobs or the rest of their body, they can get him with their eyes. Quarta has the best eyes of all of them. Completely cataract-free. Shame on her. She knows her advantage.

They begin a long, slow hiss. Quarta knows her place in their club. She knows to stay at the bottom in order to stay within the top social group. High school cool girls never disappear, they just get older and become millionaire widows.

JJ stands and begins to walk around the table toward Quarta, but Quinta steps out in front of him. Quinta is blocking his path. His view. His possibilities. JJ must handle her delicately.

"Hey, yeah," swoons Quinta. "I just wanna say that I have a kid too."

JJ wonders how high Quinta is. "Well, that's good!" he says, again all too loud.

"Hey, cool," whispers Quinta and plops into her chair like an accordion folding back into a square.

"I'm wondering," JJ begins as he approaches Quarta, "it's something that your people like to ask, and it goes something like this." JJ looks down at Quarta's melon breasts and whispers, "Where you from, eh?"

Quarta giggles. She recognizes the common question that only her own pose. She recognizes and feels a sense of home. A place far into the North that she hasn't placed her feet onto in decades.

"I'm from Iqaluit," she says. "I was born and raised there but I haven't been back in a very long time. What about you?" Quarta knows to keep his attention. She keeps her eyes locked on JJ as she draws him into the chair next to her with her chin.

"So, you're a Native woman." JJ phrases it more as a statement than a question. "I've never been with one of those." His eyes spark with curiosity. "Tell me about that. What's it like to live up there?"

"Oh, it's not as glamorous as the movies make it out to be. There's a lot of bad stuff in the North, but I can still miss it some days." Quarta takes a big swig from her glass of wine. These white guys, she thinks. These white guys and all their dumb questions. I already know what the next question will be. She takes a second swig of wine. She gives JJ her most inviting smile and calmly begins to count inside her head. Amid the numbers, the theme music for the Jeopardy final question begins to play.

"Did you ever eat raw meat?"

BINGO! thinks Quarta. He's right on target!

JJ can't stop himself from asking that common question. The question that only Inuit are asked in Canada. The question that signals their inbred lack of civilization. The question whose answer confirms what all white people think. After all, if you eat raw meat, you must be backward. Unless, of course, it is sushi.

"Yes," smiles Quarta. She moves her hand into JJ's crotch and whispers into his ear, "If I can chew and swallow that stuff, Baby, I can chew and swallow anything."

JJ nods, his eyes staying locked onto hers. He notices her heavy false eyelashes. He notices her perfectly moulded teeth with a stain of cheap lipstick on them. He notices her wide, flat tongue. The tongue that looks like all of her. Wide, flat and dull. He wasn't looking for brains and he won't have to worry about that with this one. She would be a compliant companion. A no-muss-no-fuss kind of woman. Her type know their place and require very little training. And in return you had all your wildest dreams come true.

"You certainly can!" JJ replies and leans back in his chair. He can't remember the last time he had a hard-on that mattered and was taken care of by something other than his right hand. He feels a small bump on his crotch beginning to rise like a lump of home-made bread dough in a warm bowl.

He has narrowed his choices and needs to make a decision. He seizes the moment. "If you'll excuse me, I was hoping to use the men's room." JJ scurries away before his pants embarrass him.

But JJ doesn't go to the bathroom. Instead he stands in the shadows of the lounge. He knows one thing. He knows that once he has stepped away, the members of the Rich Widows' Club will show their real selves. He stands where he can hear them, but where he knows that they can't see him. He tucks his right fist under his chin, a vertical posing of *The Thinker*. He waits for the show to unfold.

Panem et circenses, he thinks. He'd forgotten that phrase from his Latin classes until it popped back into his head a moment ago. It seems oddly appropriate for the moment: bread and circuses—that's all one needs to rule the world. He smiles wryly as he watches Prima seat herself in JJ's empty chair and lean in toward Quarta. Clearly, she has done her calculations and has chosen to re-enter the race.

"What in fuck do you think you are doing?" he sees her sneer. "You cannot be his winter travel companion! You can't. You don't have enough money to be with a guy like him. You do realize he expects you to buy your own travel insurance?"

"And not only that," adds Tertia, "he wants a woman with good hips!"

"And no previous dead husbands!" blurts Secunda. "What is it with this guy?"

"Yeah," moans Quinta. "What is it with all guys?"

Prima pushes her forked tongue to the roof of her mouth, front teeth showing. The small hiss begins. Her neck starts to flare. Her hood is slowly beginning to fill.

"We are the ones who have taught you not to shop in shopping malls!" Prima reminds Quarta. "You have a purpose in this group. Your purpose is to be our ethnic content, and you've done that very well. We've kept your brown skin and eyes around so we don't appear racist. It's politically responsible and now . . . look at you, thinking that you're somebody. Know your place!"

Quarta leans back and breaks into a chilling laugh. "You old patqut! Is that your forked tongue edging to the front of your mouth? Aren't forked tongues something that only Native people have?" Her laughter makes her cellulite tap dance up and down her big belly, causing her breasts to shake like polka dots spinning out of control on cheap fabric.

Prima strikes first. She darts her finger toward Quarta's eyes. She means for it to stop a fraction of an inch from her face, but she accidently hits a wine glass. Deftly, she flicks out her other hand to catch it, but with her attention split between the glass and her finger, the rock on her finger scrapes Quarta's cheekbone. It draws blood.

To JJ's surprise, Quarta fights back. She grips Prima's right palm, giving Prima's hand a sharp twist. The quick crackle of a green bean pops into the air. Prima's baby finger is pointed to the inside of her lifeline. Brittle bones are easy to manipulate. Osteoporosis has friends.

JJ feels a rush of adrenaline. He feels young. Their antics excite him.

Quarta takes out what looks like an EpiPen. She grins as she leans over to Prima and says in a sultry voice that hides the poison contained in her words, "Antivenom. Never leave home without it, especially when any of us are in your company, Prima."

Prima smiles back icily.

The quiver is quivering. They've never seen such a spectacle. They had entered the group knowing that Prima was the leader. Knowing that there were certain rules and expectations. They never thought that there would be an uprising. They are waiting for Quarta to bite the leader. Waiting for the change in power. Savagery arrives in many forms. They never thought it would be physical. Their wine glasses remain untouched on the table.

"He's mine!" Quarta says as she stabs the top of her left thigh. She leans back, waiting for JJ's return and the victory that she feels will almost certainly be hers.

But JJ sees something else. He can see Prima rising from her seat. She knows Quarta has overplayed her hand and has relaxed too soon. The insurrection is over, even if Quarta hasn't seen it yet. He sinks into the shadows as Prima gushes past him.

Quarta touches her cheek. She can feel the beginning of a small swelling. She takes out her Charles Mallory compact mirror and glances at herself. It won't get larger, she thinks. In the mirror,

Quarta sees the reflection of JJ's tan Brioni sweater moving toward the entrance. She turns her head and glares at JJ's escaping figure.

As JJ steps out into the sunshine, she sees Prima's limo pull up. The door opens.

JJ bows his head and steps into the vehicle.

These Old Bones

"Nobody wants these old bones," annie muttered at the early morning sunrays dipping into her living room window. She looked out onto the quiet street. The leaves were tumbling to the ground in droves. The wind was up, or as the locals called it, "the sea breeze." How did she ever end up here? On an island in the Pacific Ocean?

No friends. No man in her life except one son who never wanted her here. She knew to keep her distance from her boy. To stay away until Sunday, when they would visit over breakfast. Her life was full of time limits.

And him. Her soon-to-be ex. All those years with him. Erased. Gone. She was solo and coming up on sixty. She was living in an apartment that cost way too much, on an island almost completely alone and away from her people. It had been her great escape. Every penny that she had saved was put into this one move. The last one. The end of the road move.

No more Arctic winds. No more cold tundra. No more wondering where the next meal would come from. When she had flown away from him and his church and all the Bibles that he stacked in their tiny one-bedroom house, she had sighed the biggest sigh of relief. Finally, no more praising God or just praying for things to happen. No more people dropping in with their hearts aching and ripping and bleeding. No more having to be the good Pentecostal Wife.

She was here, stuck in the silence of her own thoughts. Stuck like a prisoner taken hostage by her one dream. To be away from all of them. From all the hurt. From all the legal battles. Away from lawyers and church people and sin and sorrow. In her mind she was free, but it was hard to be alone. Without anyone to talk to. Without anyone to hear her thoughts. Some days she wanted to scream just to be able to hear her own voice.

Some days she hungered for people. Anyone. Someone. A person to talk with. Hunger pangs that stayed deep inside of her mind's belly. Moving to a new town is not easy. It's lonely, and what brought her here were sad circumstances. Starting over when your life is in its final quarter was harder than she expected. It was pain-filled, but she told herself that it was a choice she had made and to live it for now. She told herself if it didn't work out, she could always move again. To where? She had not one clue.

She longed especially for the touch of a man's hand. She longed to feel wanted by anyone. She longed to have a man brush her hair from her cheek. To put his hand on the small of her back and steer her in the right direction. But too often the memories of him returned. How she had loved him more than anyone. How she had thought they were right for each other and then years and pain and slices of love from her heart were hung out to dry until there was no more love. The drying rack was empty.

All those years of working at staying with him. All the years that became decades of her wanting to be what was right for him. She couldn't do it any longer. She couldn't be that perfect

Pentecostal Wife. Oh, her eyes had wandered. Wandered back to the men who drank hard, who lived hard, who fucked hard. He had stopped doing all those things for his God. He had become the gentle man. His voice had turned to warm milk. His hands became as soft as puppy ears. His dick had stopped rising to any occasion.

At first, she had gone along with it all. Gone along in the way that nature had intended. But it all became too much. He stopped wanting her. He stopped sticking his tongue into any crevice of her body. When sex leaves, wives wander. When marriage becomes rooms filled with silence and arguing, it takes far too much effort and energy. That's when you know it's over, Annie thought. When she could leave the house after supper dishes were done and Moses Henry never asked her where she was going, that's when she knew she had lost him.

Lost him to the perfection of what women should be, according to the Bible. How they should serve their man first and themselves last, after having taken care of all the other family members and neighbours and the constant poor. When their boy had left home, all those years ago, she had missed the sounds of him. She missed his snoring on the couch every night at six p.m. She missed the music of him. The melody of his laugh. The song that belonged only to him.

When he was still at home, he had given them something in common. They talked about him and worried about him and waited to hear his feet on the front doorsteps late at night. Then he got the big job in the small city, and he was joyous. His face had lit up with happiness when he was leaving her behind. He was ecstatic that he no longer had to live up to everyone else's expectations. The preacher's son had flown away on the tiny Cessna and into the bigger world. She thought she would never be able to breathe again without him. In some ways she couldn't.

She felt restlessness come to her after her child had left. The house was empty. Her bed was empty. Her heart was beginning to close. Her Anaana no longer visited her. After she had married Moses Henry, her Anaana had left her. No more talking to her. No more giving her advice. The ones who go before us know there comes a time when they truly have to leave us. They wait for us instead by fires and in camps where they can visit with one another, and they still pray for us to be well as they wait to welcome us home to them.

Annie started stepping out. Heading off to the local bar. Telling herself that she would just have one. A sip of Chardonnay. Just a touch. Within a week, one had become two, and the mining men started to pay attention to her. She was well over fifty but didn't look it, feel it or act it.

She had gone to the Northern Store and bought soft red lipstick, the colour her mama used to wear. She had bought some blush, mascara, black eyeliner and a razor. She did all the things that Pentecostal women were not supposed to do. She shaved her legs. She slid the red lipstick into the curves of her mouth. She dotted her high cheekbones with blush. She let her long, dark hair slide over her square shoulders and unbuttoned the first button of her blouse. The blouse that she always wore her black bra under. She felt sexy.

Off she had gone to the bar that winter night. It was karaoke night and the locals loved it. The mining men loved watching them all stumble and try to sing, with their Northern accents turning the words into garble. Everyone laughed and it was fun. Old Johnny Cash and Merle Haggard tunes filled the bar. The words faded into the ceiling with the cigarette smoke. The crowd got drunker, and everything blended together.

That night she was brave, and she stood in front of the crowd of white men in plaid shirts and thick red beards. She put her mouth close to the mic and whispered, "I'm Annie Mukluk and I'm going to sing some Patsy Cline for you."

The men hooted and hollered and slobbered their encouragement. She felt wanted. She undid one more button on her blouse. All those years of binding submission vanished. The chains of God and rules and Commandments were loosened as she placed her red lips close to the fat microphone and began singing about walking after midnight and searching for you.

Her hips swayed just a tiny bit. She squinted her slanted eyes and looked out into the audience of men stuck in what they thought was isolation. To her it was home, and the feeling of being wanted warmed her inner thighs. It crawled up her tummy and she felt her nipples point back to every man in the crowd. It had been decades since any man had glanced at her in that way.

They were all cheering so loud that she knew they didn't hear the words she breathed into the mic. She didn't care. She felt wild. Undone. Loose. When she finished, one of the red beards lifted her off the stage and she threw her head back and flung her body forward. Laughter was spilling onto the top of his head, and then another red beard grabbed her shoulders and together the two red beards lifted her like a horizontal slab of meat. A fresh kill. One of them carried her head on his shoulder and the other held on to her small feet. She began to squirm. Fear and flight entered her bones, and she was wrestling with their grip on her. And then the crowd in the bar remembered. Remembered the chant from her early days, and they shouted in unison, "Oh Annie Muktuk, what the fuck, who did you screw last night? Oh Annie Muktuk, what the fuck, we know that you ain't tight!" Laughter zipped around the room and evil danced her out the door.

The red beards threw her to the ground, and she reached her foot up and tried to kick one of them in the crotch, but the other one slapped his thick hand across her left cheek and spun the other half of her face into the hard dirt. The buttons from her blouse popped off like firecrackers, and blood drooled its way into the corners of her lips. She was trying to scream. The scream we all have when we have nightmares. When we open our mouths, but nothing comes out no matter how hard we breathe. A red beard wrapped his hand across her teeth and told the other to hurry up and put his dick into her pussy while he ran his cock down her throat. They laughed like two old mates who had done this before.

Annie lay there broken. Split in half while their cocks jammed into her orifices. Tears slid down her face, her mascara painted black starbursts onto her eyelids. The red beards laughed and lifted her onto her knees like a rag doll.

"Here bitch, your crack is too dry. You gotta suck this one hard," the red beard hissed as he rammed his cock so far into her throat, she could not breathe. Her knees shivered, and she felt herself become robotic. She heard her thoughts tell her to just go with it. Don't resist. Follow through. They will go away. And they did. They left her on her knees, positioned like a woman in prayer.

Annie fell forward onto the earth, and finally the scream that had been stuck inside her throat with all their sperm and stink cried out into the night air. She screamed again and again, and not one person came to her side. Not one person helped her up. She managed to wrap her clothes around her small body. She limped into the night and knew that she was truly alone. She got herself to the medical clinic and begged for a rape kit. She begged to have a police officer hear her story. The nurses did their work. The cop wrote down her story. Her husband arrived and said not one word to her. He put her into the SUV and drove her home in silence. Not one word had escaped his lips in those last five years since that night. Not. One. Word. Moses Henry had stopped sleeping in her bed long before the rape. He had removed himself entirely. The rape had merely moved the inevitable one step closer.

Finally, the court date came along. The fly-in judge had listened to her testimony. Words she spoke without Moses Henry present. Words she spoke clearly and calmly. Not one tremor cracked her voice. Her lawyer had rehearsed her well. She had her story down pat, not one hesitation, not one "like" or "but" or second of silence between sentences.

When the lawyer for the defence stood, he called in people to speak to her character. They all came through the door. A lineup of white men happy to tell of their escapades with her. How they knew her from way back when. When she was so very much younger. Each one of them spoke of the sex acts they had performed with and to and on her. How she had been the best ride of their lives. Company men. All of them from so very long ago, but in the court-room it was yesterday.

An old Eskimo whore. That's what they told the judge she was as she sat there with steely eyes, memorizing their faces. The judge allowed every story. He appeared to enjoy the details. Sweat and arousal gathered on his forehead and he had to wipe it away from his brow every now and again. The stories were endless. Every time her lawyer objected, the judge would overrule and allow the testi-mony to be placed into the court records.

After all was said and done, she had lost. After waiting for five years for her case to be heard, she had lost. There was no one to side with her. No witness and no one who cared what the rape kit had shown. They walked. Her rapists. Her predators. They walked, and she was left in that tiny little Northern shithole without one person at her side. She went home. She packed her bags and sat at the airport for two days, waiting for a plane to come in to take her out. She went to her boy because he was as far away from anyone as she could get.

She ran. Ran to where no one knew her. She only had to be a stranger in a small island town. She didn't need to head up church committees or cook for people over and over again. She didn't have to put others first. She only had to be her, an Eskimo on an island.

Now, she sat on a sea-breezed island and wondered what would become of her aging self. She had come to the island, to the place where she only had to be a stranger in a small city. No one had to know her past. No one had to know her present. No one had to be in her future. She could wander through the small, narrow streets and pretend to be a tourist. She had no obligations. She had not one commitment. She did not have to answer to anyone at any time.

The mechanics of daily living set in. The first five months were spent sorting out how to live in the small town. The town where there were more white people than she had ever seen. White people with money. White people who were older than her and seemed to live forever. White and whiter. More blue eyes, more red hair. She looked for Native people. She hunted for them when she was out walking around like a tourist, attending every summer parade, walking along the waterfront. Annie counted the number of people with brown eyes and thought about making a list of how many brown-eyed people she had seen in a day and keeping a weekly tally.

The sun was different here. Hotter. It touched the earth sooner than what she was used to. Her early days were spent with setting things up. Getting a couch and chairs and a table. Putting knives and forks into kitchen drawers, trying to fill cupboards that were much taller than she was. Telling herself not to buy too many new things. New things that she may have to get rid of in the future.

She had told herself that she would only stay for as long as the money lasted. She lived small. Rarely went out. Took comfort in Netflix. Found solace in suntanning in the park and reading books. Books took her away from her daily life. Books made her focus on something other than her past.

She found joy in the plants that surrounded her. Plants that she didn't know the names of, but whose colours were beautiful. She bought far too many and lined her apartment balcony with foliage that made her happy. She walked uphill to everywhere and soon started to learn the local bus routes. She learned how to buy groceries that were different than the food she was used to. She marvelled at the abundance inside of each store. Everything was fresh. Fresh fruit. Fresh vegetables. Fresh fish. All locally grown or caught. The North had never given her this kind of choice, and now she could cook good food.

She had taken up attending Mass at an old cathedral. It felt good to fall back into Catholicism. No having to lift your hands. No having to scream out praises to a God that no one has ever seen. No having to confess to the answers to prayer or send the begging prayers for this and that out into the Western spirit world. All Annie had to do was sit in an old church and look at the stained-glass windows and look at the people around her. She had found a favourite pew. The Pew for One. When she sat there, she didn't have to mingle with the others. She didn't have to shake the "Peace be with you" salutation that every Mass asked for.

Annie always kept her Sunday appointment with her boy. The time when he talked of his week and kept certain subjects off-limits. She never spoke to him about his dad or the people back home. She never spoke to him about the past. Her contributions to each conversation were small and she kept her inner thoughts of life on an island to herself.

Instead she talked of the hummingbirds and seagulls and crows that filled her sky. Annie loved the hummingbirds best. Her balcony was on their route. There were certain flowers that they visited on her balcony every day. She knew to look for them at ten o'clock and again at two in the afternoon. She found a local store that specialized in pens and paper, and she started to draw it all. Drawings of her life in the new small town, filled with brilliant colours and soft blues.

Her days of freedom from the North. Her days of being released from Moses Henry. Her days without him, and yet she longed for the company of a man. Not a woman. Women were terrible creatures. She had never had a woman friend that she could completely trust, and she knew she never would.

When she sat in the park, countless people and their dogs were everywhere. She never talked to the dogs, because if you talked to the dogs, you would have to talk to the people who owned the dogs, and that was too much involvement. She had to remember to remain a stranger in a small town. But that one hot August day, she did something she had not done in so many years. She walked into a British-style pub and ordered a Chardonnay.

There were six large screens playing various sports, and the long counter at the bar was lined with the same people that frequented every bar she'd ever seen in real life and on TV. The old men who were somehow nailed to their stools and stuck in the same place every day by three in the afternoon. The same men who had lived their lives inside of the same bar since their teens.

Men who were her age or older represented problems. Health problems that went on and on and never stopped. Or money problems and the problems of retirement and what that would cost them. Problems. That's all they were. Problems. Men without erections who took their tiny pool of aging testosterone elsewhere. To their bank accounts, to their workouts at the gym, to their tireless hours seated at bars, talking about life in 1968.

Men without testosterone who found power in persuasion. They lured in younger women and talked a good game until push came to shove. Then they shoved hard and real and knocked that woman square onto her ass and then sat back and claimed innocence. Claimed misinterpretation. Claimed that the woman had wanted what they had not. Old men. Old men without charm, balding like weak eagles on rocky cliffs.

Annie knew all that. Knew what the old white men were about, and she sat there and sipped her wine and thought about what to watch on Netflix that night. One man with a white goatee and an even whiter hat looked at her from across the bar, caught her eye and shouted, "You are a remarkable-looking woman!" Annie grinned and looked down at the bar counter.

He came close to her and introduced himself. "I'm Alex, and you are?"

"Annie."

"Annie, what a lovely name. Where are you from?"

"Oh, up North. Quite a distance from here."

"And where would that be? Churchill or some place like that? You look Native. Are you one of those, you know, what do they call them . . . Eskimos!"

Annie felt her shoulders start to tighten. She gave a half-smile and a half-nod.

"Really! Hey fellas, look over here—it's an Eskimo!"

She knew not to interact. No matter what. Not with a white guy, and especially not with an old white guy. She let her breath out and held her head up a little higher.

"Like the football team, you mean, Alex?" The bar burst into hard laughter. Peals of it slip-sliding everywhere. Annie saw the bellies of all those white men jiggling like Mr. Claus. She saw their white beards ho-ho-ing and their blue eyes glittering like the stars on a Christmas tree. Annie saw what she always saw in white men. Annie saw hate.

She turned her head away from the man named Alex and nodded to the bartender that she wanted to pay her bill.

"Oh, now don't run off," said Alex, his white teeth lining the edges of his white goatee. "Sit with me for a while and tell me about yourself. Now what is it that they call you people nowadays? In-you-ette. In-you-ite?"

"In-you-pants!" shouted another of the Bar Flies, and again the room roared.

Annie stared into his diamond-blue eyes and shook her head: No. She was trying to get up from her stool when Alex put the fingers from his right hand into the small of her back. Annie felt the pressure on the base of her spine, and she felt the snarl begin to rise from her throat.

"I'm leaving," Annie said barely above a whisper. "I'm leaving."

"Oh, now you can't do that, dear Annie. Sit with this old gent and tell me the story of being an Eskimo in Canada. The one thing I want to know is, do you really eat raw meat?"

"Alex, those Eskimo women eat all meat. Raw, red and hard!" shouted another of the Bar Flies, and the laughter started to roll back and forth, up and down the bar counter again.

Annie reached behind her back and grabbed Alex's fingers. She squeezed them together tight and sneered, "You old white fuck. I'm leaving."

"Whoa now girl, you don't get to talk to me like that!" exclaimed Alex as he reached for her waist with both of his hands, pressing hard into her stomach. "There now, settle down. Steady it a bit, girl!"

Annie pulled Alex's hands off her belly and pushed her arms straight back as hard as she could. The hard tips of her elbows landed on Alex's ribs and she heard his breath pop out of him. Annie turned to leave while a man in the bar started to hoot and holler, "You got a live one, Alex. Ride 'em, cowboy!"

She felt Alex's hand pull on her right arm, and she swung her purse toward him as hard as she could. She felt the rage inside of her bubble and boil over. She felt the hate that she had had for white men crawl down her arms and sit on her nails. She wanted to scratch this fucker's eyes out.

Annie swung her arm back one more time. Her purse flew through the air. The Bar Flies were laughing and chanting, "Go Alex, go!" when she heard a voice break into her ears behind her.

"Trouble follows you everywhere, doesn't it?"

She would have recognized that voice anywhere, everywhere and at any time of day or night.

Annie turned and looked into the eyes of Johnny Cochrane. The man in this world who hated her most.

The man who would be so thrilled to have his Moses Henry back to himself.

Johnny placed his face in front of Alex's and hissed, "Listen, you soft white piece of shit, you leave my woman alone. You white boys need to know your place. Get back to your bar stool." Alex backed up, back to the bar stool that had been his for over five decades.

Johnny turned to Annie and smiled. He reached out his hand and nodded. Annie's trembling hand locked with his, and they walked out of the pub together.

Once they were outside, Annie started to shake and shake. She couldn't stop herself. She felt the tears welling up into pools in the corner of each eye, and no matter how hard she tried to blink them away, they fell like huge raindrops onto the sidewalk.

"I'm sorry, Johnny," she said between gasps. "I'm so sorry. Thank you. Ma'na."

Johnny grinned his timeless grin and asked, "You hungry? I know a little place not far from here, closer to the water, and they have the best salmon dinner. I call that place 'Swan-a-licious.' You ever been there?"

"I don't go out, Johnny. This was the first time I stepped into a bar in this place. And the last. I'm sorry. I have to go back to my place. I can't eat. I can't think. I have to go."

Annie walked up the sidewalk as fast as she could, but Johnny stayed by her side as though he was out on an evening stroll. Johnny stepped out in front of her and did something that Annie thought he would never do.

Johnny Cochrane wrapped his arms around her shoulders and folded Annie into his chest. She let out the longest howl of sorrow. They created one crooked and sideways Inukshuk as they cried together on a street filled with tourists.

They cried for all the hate they had felt from the world. They cried for all the hate they had had for each other all those years up North. They cried together because they were the two people who knew what it was like to lose the love of Moses Henry.

Johnny pulled his face back from hers. He did what we all do when our emotions tell us to get some control. He burst out laughing. Annie joined him. When they had laughed themselves out, they wiped the wetness from their faces onto the sleeves of their shirts.

Johnny asked again, "Dinner?" and put his right arm out for Annie to latch onto.

They walked in silence down the streets of the small city. No words were shared between them, and when they arrived at the restaurant, Johnny gallantly pulled the chair back for Annie.

Then he pointed up to the top of the wall and said, "Madam, you are seated in what I call The Pierre Chair. Our former prime minister will be dining with us tonight." Annie looked up and smiled at the portrait of Pierre Trudeau, who was looking down at them with a softness in his eyes.

"Seems like life was easier when we had that guy around, don't you think?"

Johnny shrugged and smiled his big smile. The smile that had got him in and out of bed with so many women. Johnny Cochrane may have had his hair turn a shade of grey, but that grin had never left him. He was charm. He was handsome. He was magic.

"Oh, we always think that the old days were good, but were they really?" Johnny asked. The waitress approached, and Johnny turned on his charm. Within five minutes he had ordered a bottle of Chardonnay, found out the name of the waitress, what time her shift was over and where he could find her at eleven at night. Annie sat across from him, shaking her head and smiling.

"Some things never change," she said.

"No, they don't," Johnny grinned. "No, they don't. What are you doing here?"

"Me? What are you doing here?" Annie asked with a giggle.

"Been out this way for a decade now. Got a nice, comfy government job that I retired from. Now I just spend my days saving damsels in distress. Tell me, what are you doing here?"

"Johnny, I . . ." and Annie couldn't find the words she wanted. "I came here to be close to my boy."

"No, you didn't," said Johnny. "Tell me what really happened."

"The rape. The rape happened. And then he was completely gone from me. Oh, he had left long before the rape. He wasn't anywhere near me for decades. Decades. But the rape was the last straw."

Johnny reached his hand across the table and put it on hers. He squeezed it tight and nodded. "I know. I heard about the rape. I'm sorry, Annie. I'm sorry that happened to you, and I'm sorry for all the terrible things I said about you when we were younger. You never deserved it. You never did."

Annie pulled her hand back from his and looked out at the street. Cyclists everywhere, the big new bridge looking shiny and strong, the water off in the distance.

"I lost him, Johnny. I lost him so long ago, and why did I ever think that I could be a preacher's wife? Me of all the fucking people on this earth being a preacher's wife. How dumb was I?

"But we had our boy, and he kept us together for all those years, and then he left. And I don't know what happened to me. I got restless. I got lonelier. I got tired of the silence in my own house. I never should have gone out that night. Just like I should not have gone out tonight. It was happening all over again . . . thank god for you. Thank god for you appearing and saving me. I was so terrified."

Johnny raised his wineglass and smiled. "To you Annie Mukluk. A survivor."

Annie smiled back and felt a certain peace pass over her body. She was in a brief pocket of comfort. She was with one of her own.

ANNIE NOW KNEW TWO PEOPLE ON THIS ISLAND, HER BOY AND Johnny, but she didn't want to burden them. She didn't want to seem needy for anything, although she longed for their company. She longed to talk to them. To go out somewhere with them. But she kept to herself. Kept to her daily walks. Kept to taking pictures of all the odd shops and different things she found on that island, like the community book exchanges—things that looked like bird houses but were packed with books. She read every book that was placed in the exchange close to her home and put it back when she was done.

Johnny did text her every day. Small little lines telling her what he was doing. "Going for groceries in Langford!" or "Down at the dock!" She texted back as few encouraging words as possible. She was terrified of seeming forward, of needing someone's time, of displaying the complete loneliness that engulfed her very being. She would not appear that way. Instead she texted back, "On Broughton! Have fun!" or "Looking at fish for tonight's supper. Have the best day!" Those few words were her only communication with the outside world. There were days when not one sound escaped her throat. There were days when she longed to hear herself speak.

One morning, the text from Johnny read, "Want to walk on the breakwater?" Annie felt the excitement inside herself. She texted back, "Yes! What time?" and began to prepare for her big day, her big event of walking with someone instead of alone. She took the bus downtown and started to walk in the direction that she thought the breakwater was, but she had to stop and ask for directions. She saw Johnny walking a few yards ahead of her but didn't shout out to him. She walked along behind him, grinning at his swagger.

The swagger he always walked with back home. It suited him here. The only thing missing was the sound of the spurs he used to wear up home. His long ponytail was now a short buzz cut. The buzz suited him, too. Men aged better than women. They just did. Annie could have called out for him to stop, but she liked watching him from behind. The way he stopped and looked over at some people's flowers or bent down and scratched a dog's ears. She thought about how much more relaxed he was here. Maybe she would find that too.

He was sitting on a bench, waiting, when she arrived. He was talking with some people, so Annie stayed back a bit longer. She didn't want to interrupt. She didn't want to be an interruption to anyone's life. She had been trained to stay back. Finally, she walked up to him with a big smile, happy for the company of another person. They walked together along the breakwater, the wind pressing their T-shirts and shorts tight against their bodies and the sun turning their brown skins browner.

"You look good, Annie," Johnny said. She smirked and shook her head. "Well, you know what I mean—for an old lady your age!" Annie slapped Johnny's hip and reminded him that he was older than she was.

"You ever get married, Johnny?" Annie asked. She had always wanted to know if he had done that. The one thing she could never imagine him doing.

"Yep, that lasted all of five seconds," Johnny said with a laugh. "Don't think I was cut out for monotony . . . I mean, monogamy. Not my thing, but I gave it a try."

"Kids?"

"Zero. Best thing that came out of that relationship was zero population growth. My contribution to climate control. It was sad for me, though. I think I loved her, but it just didn't work out in the way it should have. You? You got a boyfriend?"

"Me?" Annie was shocked. "I was telling myself the other day that no one wants these old bones, and I'm pretty sure of that."

"You're still fine, Annie. Geez, get out there and see what's snaking around this town!"

"Think I had my fill at that pub. Not doing that again."

They stood, looking out at the sea. Eventually, Johnny spoke. "You hear from him?"

"Never. Not one word. He hasn't talked to me in years, and I mean years. I never measured up. I never could."

"Well, that's one thing we have in common. I didn't measure up either. Not for him. All those years of saving his sorry ass in day school, and now he can't be bothered to even pick up the phone. God's got him and got him good."

"And your mom?"

"Oh, I have her tucked away in a home here. Nice place, and she's doing okay for a woman who nearly drank her liver away. Here, let's sit on this bench and look at the Tudor house across the way— can you imagine growing up in that? Close to the water and all this beauty. Wouldn't that have been a dream? Watching big ships pass by and thinking about all those people from foreign countries coming to town. So different from what we had, eh?" Johnny chuckled that winning chuckle she remembered.

Annie didn't realize it at first, but she had put her arm around Johnny's shoulders. It was funny, her sitting there with her arm around the one guy from home who had hated her more than anyone in the entire community.

"Sorry!" she sputtered as she realized what she was doing. "Sorry! I didn't mean to touch you. God, I'm such a social idiot!"

Johnny pulled her hand back across his shoulders. "Leave it there. It feels nice. That's the one thing about being alone, eh—the lack of touch. I think about booking myself in for a massage just to have someone touch me."

"Hey, come on, you're Johnny Cochrane—every girl in town wants to touch you!"

"I don't want to touch them. You look at the stuff this town has. The Old Ones. Man, I've met some real losers with tons of money and enough plastic surgery to make you think they're wearing a clown's mask! Dog Fucking Ugly. And the young ones . . . Well, they think you've got money and that's why they come around. Nope. I have a pretty quiet life out here."

"Completely celibate, Johnny?"

"Well, not completely. I have this one friend. She's from my old days in university in Winnipeg. You know, when I was busy getting my MA degree. She's here, and we spend time together. Go for walks and talk and she comes by and we play crib or Scrabble—stuff like that."

"And that's all?"

"Well, I don't kiss her!"

"Most whores don't allow kissing."

"She's not a whore. She's, you know, just someone."

"Why aren't you all in with her?"

"She's married."

"She's monotonous."

They both burst out laughing, and Annie felt fine. It was good to hear someone else's story of how they survive out here on the island. To hear that loneliness didn't belong only to her.

"You should never go near married stuff. Never. Not a good gig, Johnny. But hey, I'm not here to judge, and if having Miss Married drop by once a week works for you, then good for you. Are you ever gonna fuck her brains out?"

Johnny shrugged, "I don't know. I think that's coming, though, and I don't know if I want that with her or anyone ever again. Just don't think I can do that thing called 'relationship.' But this is getting too deep and too dull. Let's go grab a bottle of wine and find a beach!"

"Johnny Cochrane, you still know how to worm your way into a woman's heart." Annie stood and took his hand. They walked back toward the restaurant at the other end of the breakwater. Two displaced, heartbroken Eskimos walking down a long slab of cement, something put there by man, not by nature. They were the breakwater.

Later, they watched the sun diving down past the ocean and into the deep of space. It had been a good day. It had been a good walk. A good talk. They had eaten hamburgers together. They had shared a bottle of wine. They had put their toes into water that was different from what they grew up with. They had hugged each other good night at the bus stop.

Annie got into her bed with a smile that night. It had been the best day.

A few days later, they were winding and whirling along on the road to Pedder Bay. Laughing and telling each other stories about the people back home. The sun was unusually warm, and a small breeze blew up from the ocean.

"Do you remember that guy, No Nose?" Johnny was shifting gears constantly on the road that twirled and twirled. Moving from third to second gear and back up to fourth when the road straightened out just a bit.

"Yeah, I remember him. Such a sad story his is."

"Why do you feel bad for him? Geez, he went on to set the Guinness World Record for longest living man without nostrils! Something like a hundred thousand dollars! If I had known that blowing your nose off instead of your brains out got you that kind of cash, I woulda done it!"

"Johnny, that's really not funny. I mean, think about it. Think what he lives with. I hear that when he swallows food, parts of it come out his nose."

"Think of what it's like to have that sitting across from you at Christmas dinner. Peas, carrots, potatoes . . . all dripping back into his plate and him eating it over and over again."

Annie burst out laughing. She laughed until her ribs ached. It felt good to laugh. It felt good to have someone to laugh with. She looked over at Johnny Cochrane and smiled. He was handsome. He had never stopped being handsome. He had that personality that made everyone love him somehow.

"And here we are. My dear Annie, you are about to be introduced to the world's worst boat. A sixteen-foot aluminum thing that is older than dirt, and we will go out onto the water in it and get us a big salmon, and tonight—fresh fish for dinner!"

Annie and Johnny walked down to the dock, each of them carrying a pile of fishing rods and life jackets and plastic pails.

"We sure didn't have all this stuff when we were kids fishing back home, did we?" Annie remarked.

"Hell no, girl! We just grabbed a rod, jumped into the boat and fired up the motor! No fuss, and like my mama used to say, 'No sweat in the Arctic!' Man, she used to make me feel good when she said that. When she was sober."

Johnny started up the boat and they chugged their way out into the ocean, the boat gently rocking them up and down. In the distance, they could see the big ships loaded with containers of goods, looking strong and mighty. They passed by a group of otters diving into the water from the shore and swirling around on their backs.

"Look!" Annie shouted with far too much glee. "Otters! Johnny did you know that when they sleep, they hold hands? Isn't that beautiful? Just think of that, having someone hold your hand every night when you're sleeping."

"I never thought of you as a romantic, Annie, and I would want someone holding a different body part every night of my life." Annie shook her head and let her hair fly about her face.

Johnny studied her. Thought how gorgeous she was. You wouldn't guess she was coming up on sixty. Maybe forty-five. All that long, dark hair and the perfect nose and full lips. She made him think of the good parts of home. The good people. The good food. The way their own laughed easy and hard over almost nothing.

He wondered how Moses Henry could have let her go. All these decades later Johnny could see the beauty that was inside of Annie. She was like a little girl in so many ways.

"What? What are you looking at? Do I have crap on my face? You know I'm the worst eater. Had yogurt for breakfast. It's on my face, isn't it?" Annie wiped away at her chin and ran the back of her hand over her mouth.

"No, nothing on your face, Annie. I was just thinking about home. You make me think about the good parts of it. You do."

Annie blushed and looked away. Then she looked back into Johnny's dark eyes and smiled. "We gonna get those rods out into the water or bounce across the water thinking of someplace else?"

"You're all work today, miss. Here, I'll prop the poles into the stands."

"Stands? That's how you fish—just stick rods into stands? That's not real fishing. Here, let me put one out into the water."

"We aren't pulling in pickerel here, Annie. We're in about a hundred and forty feet of water, and we're hoping for the big one. Wahooo! My line is pulling!" Johnny cut the motor on the boat and pulled the rod that had arched into an upside-down U out of its holding stand. The line stretched, and Johnny pulled and wound the spool. Pull and wind. Pull and wind. Johnny and the fish fighting it out.

Annie watched Johnny's strong arms, watched his mouth tighten, watched his hands tremble like those of a little boy on Christmas morning.

"Grab the net!"

"What? No!"

"Grab the net. I'm going to pull him along the right side here. Put the net into the water. Hurry!" Annie grabbed the green net by the handle and put it into the water.

"I think you should do this."

"I can't! I gotta move the fucker over your way. Man, he's heavy. We got 'im. A big one!"

"Johnny, this is too much pressure. If I don't get him in the net, you lose your fish and . . ."

"Ssh. Here he comes. Make sure he goes in head-first. There, he's in. Now lift him. Lift!"

Annie pulled as hard as she could and turned the net handle over to Johnny. "I can't. He's too heavy."

Johnny put his rod onto the floor of the boat and lifted the big fish into the air. The big salmon flip-flopped inside the net as Johnny gently placed it onto the bottom of the boat. Johnny let out a huge hurray and grabbed Annie by the waist. He hugged her close and said, "Kiss?"

Annie put her face forward and allowed him to give her a small peck, but Johnny pulled her in closer and softly placed his lips against hers. He let them linger there. It was pure heaven. The fish slapped its tail hard against Johnny's ankle in approval. Annie and Johnny felt a small splash fly up toward them.

They pulled away from one another. When they got back to shore, Johnny carried his big fish up to the weighing station. He was proud, and Annie was enjoying his happiness. Johnny slid the bottom lip of the salmon onto the big hook. It weighed just over fifteen pounds. Johnny felt like a champ as Annie took photo after photo. A young blonde woman came along and asked, "Is that a real fish?"

Annie held her hand tight against her mouth to stop her laugh from falling out. Johnny looked over calmly and said, "Yes, ma'am, that's a real fish."

"Oh, wow! Can I, like, take a picture of it?"

"Go right ahead." Johnny looked over at Annie and winked.

When they were driving back to the small town, Johnny was talking politics. He was talking racism. He was talking about every serious thing that the news tells the world to think about every night at six. Every time he would get into a rant, Annie would look at him and say, "Johnny, I just want to know one thing. Was that a real fish?" And they would both break into laughter.

Johnny Cochrane was driving along, laughing and watching Annie's hair fly around the cab of his truck. Johnny Cochrane had not had this much fun in a very long time. He reached over and grabbed Annie's hand and held it tight.

Annie looked back, confused and a little bewildered. She leaned across her seat and kissed his cheek, turned her head to look out the side window. She did not pull her hand away.

After supper, they sat on Johnny's balcony and watched the last rays of sun go away. Their stomachs were filled with fresh fish and vegetables. They felt the glow and relaxing effect of the wine seep into them.

"That was a good day," Annie said. "Thank you, Johnny."

"I thank you for spending the day with me. It was fun."

"Well, I think I should call a cab and head back to my loneliness," Annie said as the dark enveloped them. Johnny shook his head and motioned for her to sit down.

"What? Do you need something?"

"Just stay a while longer, Annie."

Annie sat down again.

"Do you think we should try to get a hold of him?" Johnny asked after a long silence. "You know, call him and just see how he's doing."

"He's fine in his own little world," Annie said. "The people up there love him, and he'll be taken care of for the rest of his days. Now, I have to find my cell and call a cab."

"No, I mean, shouldn't we let him know that we're both here."

"Because why? What would it matter if he knew we were both here?"

"If he finds out from someone else, Annie, he'll think you came here for me."

Annie looked at Johnny and burst out laughing. "As if, Johnny. As if I came here for you. Geez, you're a nice guy and everything, but I doubt that even Moses Henry would think that!"

"Come on, Annie, he knows what I thought about you all those years ago. You know, I always had these thoughts about you and how, you know, if you and I ever got it on . . ."

Annie did not know. Annie had never known. Johnny continued awkwardly. "Well, you know, we're cut from the same cloth in that area and all that."

"The same cloth? Johnny, this is stupid talk. This is wine talk. I'm calling my cab, and I'll wait for it downstairs." Annie turned to leave, but Johnny held her hand.

"Didn't you ever think about me that way?" Johnny asked sincerely. "Really, Annie, never?"

"Johnny, listen, I may have been a crazed little sex machine all those decades ago. Remember, I said decades ago, so don't you go getting any ideas now, mister. I'll admit that I was a bit of a wild child, but you were the enemy. So, no, I never thought of you like that. Never."

"Really, you didn't? Geez, I was hot back then, Annie. You should have thought of me like that. Look at all the women I was with."

"And look at all the guys I was with. I mean, none of them mattered. I liked treating them as though I was on a good hunt and coming in for the kill. Ah, that's decades ago, and this is stupid talk. Let's call it a day."

They hugged each other one more time. Annie turned and blew a kiss Johnny's way as she stepped into the cab. Johnny pretended to catch it and smacked his hand against his lips.

That night, Annie lay in bed trying to figure out why she had never thought about Johnny that way. Why had she never tried to get him into bed the way she had all the other men who were in town. Why had she never been attracted to him. Was she attracted to him now? she wondered. She didn't think so.

He came into her dream that night. The dream that had haunted her for so very long. The dream that had kept her medicated until she left the North. Antidepressants through the day and Zopiclone through the night. That was how she had got by after the rape. She had lived a life of no feeling. No feeling sad. No feeling mad. No feeling anything. The drugs kept her in a zone of nothingness. When she had moved to the small town, she had stopped all of it. No more feeling nothing, but now the feelings had come in so intense and sleep had become her nemesis. The hardest thing she did was try to sleep. That's why she walked and walked every day. She tried to walk her way into exhaustion. She tried to walk her way into sleep.

The red beards began to appear again at night. They would laugh as they grabbed at her breasts and pulled on her pubic hair. They had the teeth of wolverines, which they bared every time they wrestled with her. All three of them on a cloud above the ocean and the two red beards assaulting her. She wrestled and fought and hit at them, but they laughed even harder. They would turn her over onto her belly and fuck her from behind doggy-style and laugh the entire time.

Tonight, Johnny appeared with a spear in his right hand and he stabbed at them over and over again. There was blood everywhere and she was crying out to him. Johnny finished them off and came over to her. He cuddled her nakedness and rocked her gently in his arms. He lifted her face to his and kissed her.

She sat up straight in her bed, the sweat pouring off her. What did that dream mean? She grabbed her pen and the paper and started to draw it all out. The red beards and their teeth, the cloud, the water underneath and Johnny to the side with his spear. She drew the dream sequence and sat back on her pillows. What did it mean?

Early the next morning, Annie sent a text to Johnny: "J: I need to see your mom. Can I?"

Johnny read the text and didn't reply. He didn't like it. People getting into his business. It was his business. His mom was his business. Some days she was good, but not often. Her mind could barely remember five minutes ago. How could Annie expect his mom to remember her? And if she did remember Annie, absolutely none of it would be kind. Not. One. Bit.

Johnny's phone rang. It was Annie. He held the phone in his hands and debated whether to answer or not. "Ah shit," he said and pressed the green button.

"Hello?" Johnny said. "How are you doing today, Annie?"

"Johnny, I'm sorry. I know you don't like people calling you, but I've been having these nightmare things and I wanted to talk to your mom about them."

"She's not a gypsy with a crystal ball looking in the future, Annie, and she's not so good . . ."

"Well, I've drawn them, and I just want her to look at them. Johnny, I gotta talk to one of our own. She knows the old ways like we don't, and you know she would know what to tell me. Please. Even just once. Please."

"Annie, she might not recognize you. She has days when she doesn't even recognize me, and it's important for her to stay calm."

Johnny sounded as though he was pleading with her. "And besides, she's my business. My stuff. I mean, I owed her something after I left her up there, and now, well, now she's okay and she's quiet and I'd like to keep her that way."

"Just think about it, Johnny. Just think about letting me visit with her. Can you do that much?" Annie didn't mean to sound ungrateful. She didn't mean to sound like she was being demanding. She didn't want to upset the only other grown-up that she knew on the island.

Johnny let her words sit with him for a while before he spoke. "All right. Just once. I can pick you up at one o'clock and take you there."

"Ma'nallunav'juaq."

"Now you're just talking dirty to me, Annie." She could hear the laughter in his voice.

"Johnny, stop."

"Takuturaunniarvuguk—See you later, alligator!"

Johnny met her outside her place and drove her to his mother's. They stopped in front of a castle. It was white with blue trimming. Soft blue like the water it pointed out at. Annie could not believe what she was seeing. This was the fanciest nursing home on earth. When Annie and Johnny entered the foyer, a chandelier sparkled at them and a butler in what looked like a tuxedo bowed at them.

"This is where your mom is?" Annie whispered into Johnny's ear. He nodded.

"Wow. This is the Ritz of nursing homes! I smell chlorine. Is there a pool here? Do you swim in it?"

"Annie, shhh. We'll take the elevator up to mom's room."

The elevator was a mirrored contraption and yet another, smaller chandelier lit their way up to floor twenty. When they stepped out, glassed walls showed them the ocean water, the waves rocking in perfect rhythm on the beach below.

"Holy smokes! This must cost a fortune!" Annie couldn't contain herself. Again, Johnny looked at her and put his right index finger to his lips. They walked down the thick-carpeted hallway. Annie's feet felt like they were walking on an angel food cake. Spongy. Soft and comforting. Johnny tapped lightly on door twenty-one.

She heard a voice call, "Come in," and Johnny slowly opened the door.

"Mama, Anaana. It's me, Johnny. I brought a friend today. Do you remember Annie from up home?"

Johnny's mom sat in a wheelchair and turned her head toward Annie. She looked confused, and then the recognition of who Annie was began to spread across her eyes.

She smiled and tapped at the chair next to her. "My girl. Have a seat. It's always good to see someone from home. Here, sit. Johnny, go make us some tea." Johnny looked at Annie and shrugged and headed off to the kitchen.

"Mrs. Cochrane, it's so good to see you too. How have you been? How do you like living in these fancy digs?" Annie smiled and reached over to hold Mrs. Cochrane's hand. She felt the dryness of it and the wrinkles that crackled along the edges of the ancient tan-coloured palm. Somehow, she felt like she was in the presence of her own mom. As though her mom's spirit had entered the room with them.

"You were the naughty girl." Mrs. Cochrane's voice crackled with delight. Annie blushed and turned her face toward the ocean view.

"Yep. That was what everyone said." Annie kept her eyes down toward the angel food cake carpet that had followed them into the suite.

"Hey, now, my girl," Annie felt a light tap on her chin. "Look up here. That was years ago, and we all know how people up North run their mouths about everyone and everything. Now tell me, what are you doing here. Living so far from home. You like my Johnny and wanted to find a warmer place?"

"Partly. Bad stuff happened and I left. My boy is here too, and I guess I had no place else to run to, so I came here. And then I ran into Johnny a few weeks ago and asked him if I could come see you. I hope you don't mind."

"Mind! I'm happy for the company. Johnny always tries to be a good boy, and he put me into this high-falutin' place. They call this castle a home for old people, but it's more like a warehouse of death." Mrs. Cochrane laughed. She had the laugh of a poker player who had just won the jackpot. It was infectious.

"I was hoping you could look at some drawings that I've made, Mrs. Cochrane, and tell me what you think. Only if you want to, that is."

"Now don't rush along, my girl. Johnny!" she hollered, "How's that tea coming?"

"It's done, Mama. I'll be out in a second."

"It's fun to hear someone boss that guy around." Annie looked at Mrs. Cochrane. Her eyes had the flecks that start to fill up around the pupils as we age. The dark patches of wisdom that bodies create as they look out onto the world in a person's final years.

Johnny brought out the tea on a silver tray. Cookies covered the old country rose design on the Royal Albert plate.

"I love this china," sighed Annie. "I always wanted to have some china and would dream of it up home. One time I found an old teacup with this pattern. It makes tea taste better, don't you think?"

Mrs. Cochrane giggled. "See Johnny, these are things girls talk about. So many times, I wished I'd had a daughter. For now, Annie, and for as long as you live here, you'll be my girl."

Annie felt comfortable. It was all surreal. This feeling of comfort and caring that washed through her. She wished she could sit with Mrs. Cochrane forever. The three of them sipped their tea and talked. Mrs. Cochrane talked about the latest gossip from home. How she had heard the Northern Store was selling legal marijuana and how that would make things worse up there. Mrs. Cochrane mentioned Moses Henry only once. Said she had heard that he was seen around town with a white woman. Annie flinched.

"Well, I'm gone, and he can do whatever he pleases," she said. "He owes me nothing, Mrs. Cochrane. Not one thing, and we had a good marriage for a while."

"The first two years are always good, my girl—it's the next fifty that stink!"

Annie finally took her drawing pad out of her bag. She placed it on Mrs. Cochrane's lap and told her she was welcome to flip through it. Mrs. Cochrane and Johnny both were stunned at the drawings of the hummingbirds and seagulls and the flowers that made you sure that you could smell them on the page. They praised her work over and over again until they came to a final sequence of drawings.

The red beards. The naked lady with long, dark hair. The man with the spear in the clouds. Blood splattered everywhere. Dark violence on the page.

Mrs. Cochrane gasped. She held her crooked fingers tight to her lips. She started to cry. Tight tears against her pinched mouth. A moan of desperation. Mrs. Cochrane shook her head and handed the pad back to Annie. Annie reached out her hand and squeezed Mrs. Cochrane's palm in hers.

"I'm sorry. I didn't know."

Johnny reached across and wrapped his mother's shoulders up with one arm and glared over at Annie. "This is why. This is why you can't come here," he said in the quietest whisper.

"No, no, Johnny. It's time I tell the story. The story of you."
Mrs. Cochrane drew in a long breath and let it slide slowly out of
her from between her teeth. The hiss of remorse.

"When I was a young lady, like that one with the long hair in
your picture, I fell in love with a red beard. Oh, I loved a man that
I knew I should not have. I knew he was white and that red colour
on him was all the anger that came out of him every day. The anger
that painted him red. Red hair all over his body. Even on his back
it was like thick fur and not soft fur. Hard fur. I went off with him.
Took off South, and I met his brother.

"His brother had the red hair too, but his red hair was like a passion. A passion that was filled with love for the earth. For life. For
being alive. I don't even want to tell how it happened, but eventually I was sleeping with both of them. Not under one roof like in the
old times when an Inuit woman had more than one husband. I'd
sneak here and there."

Mrs. Cochrane stopped and crushed her eyelids together tight
and drained her tear ducts. She did not wipe the tears from her
cheeks. Johnny leaned in and brushed them away tenderly.

"Mama, don't talk. It's okay. I don't need to know anything."

"They were the men who fathered you and your twin. They were
the ones who were your dads. See there in the picture Annie drew."
Her bent fingers swirled around the man in the clouds. "That's you."

"But he has a harpoon, Mama. I never touched one."

"I had twins, and your brother killed himself. I always knew you
would be the one who lived on. I always knew that even before he
was found dangling off the dock . . . for me it was not a surprise. I
knew that in the end, you would be the one to care for me."

Johnny hugged her hard, and together they cried the way that
only a mother and son know how to. The way a mother adores her

boy all the days of his life. The longest, strongest bond a man will ever have is with his mother. Wives can't change that.

Annie moved her weight from one hip to the other. Back and forth. Forth and back. She didn't want to interrupt. This moment was theirs. It wasn't about her or the red beards back home.

It wasn't about rape. It wasn't about hate. Perhaps she had been dreaming about love.

She was seeing a side of Johnny that she didn't know was alive. She was seeing a Johnny Cochrane who could show love. Maybe the dreams were meant to bring her here to this. To see Johnny in a different way. Not the guy swaggering down a sidewalk with spurs on his boots. Not the guy with wild hair-washing parties. This Johnny Cochrane had aged into gentleness.

"Now, Johnny, you know I love you," Mrs. Cochrane whispered, "but I need to make a call. You go get the cordless phone. I have to call Isadore."

"Mama, who is Isadore?"

"Isadore Stanley. He's a Métis artist who lives down the hall. I want him to see Annie's drawings."

"And how do you know him, Mama?"

"He's the artist-in-residence this year, and you know what? He's hot!"

"Oh, my Gawd, my mother is back!" Johnny and his mama burst out laughing. Falling over laughter. Laughter you never want to have stop. The kind that makes you walk away from one another because you can't stand the ache of it all. When they had finished laughing, Johnny went to get the phone.

The days flew by. The seasons changed bit by bit. On the island, the seasons seemed to move slower. Leaves took longer to change colour. Leaves took longer to drop to the ground. Leaves took longer to roll up and crunch when you stepped on them. Island life was filled with leisurely humidity.

Annie kept drawing and drawing and walking and walking. Isadore Stanley took her on as an art student, and soon her work was being displayed in local shops and restaurants. Her hummingbirds and flowers sold and sold. She started to make a bit of money. Enough to keep her afloat. After a year, she had found a bit of contentment. She had routine to her days and a few treasured friends. Mrs. Cochrane was one of those treasures.

She never told anyone about her past. Only Johnny and his mom knew what had happened. And her boy. They knew the pain never really went away. It only faded a tiny bit and returned with sharp pangs on days she didn't want it to.

Tainna
(The Unseen Ones)

Billy townsend slid his skinny ass onto the john deere lawnmower. It was still a bit dark out, leaving the early spring morning air heavily scented with dew. He loved that smell. One of the best things about his job was being able to head out onto the golf course and drive the mower in the early morning.

After three decades of military assignments that scattered his life with time zones, this early morning duty was his simplest. He had finally reached that point in his life where he could relax at work, something he had never been able to do when serving his country. Today was the first mowing of the greens for the season. One of his favourite days. He knew it would be a long day, but the first mow was always the best mow.

He had seen it all during his years of service. So many cold nights during Desert Storm, so many hot, sweltering days when you begged God for a breeze—and when it came, it was loaded with sand that would seep its way into every crack of your body. Every line on his face. He put in those final years and got the hell out. Out onto Civvy Street, where his biggest concern was getting through the Tim Hortons drive-thru on his way to work. It was a simple life now.

He liked the routine of his days. The hum and flow of life without others to answer to. Each spring, summer and early fall, all he did was "mow da lawn." He smiled as he thought of his French military buddies making fun of him and calling him "Billy Mow DaLawn." He hummed in time with his mower motor as he headed off toward the first green. Cresting the small hill, he looked down upon a flock of Canada geese sitting in a circle.

Sitting in a circle with their necks pointing outwards. Sitting like bison do when protecting their young against aggressors. Billy couldn't believe his eyes. He put his mower into stealth mode and moved silently toward the geese.

There must be sixty of them, he thought. He had never seen this formation. He had never seen geese behave like this. Not that he was a hunter. Not that he really understood nature, but he knew a bit of this and that. And of this he was certain: geese did not sit in bison circles.

He eased his mower toward the circle. Not one of the geese moved. Not one goose let loose a honk. Not one of them lifted its head from under its wing. Billy didn't understand it. He was confused. He felt like he was in a bad dream where everything falls in slow motion. He touched his left pocket to make sure he had his cellphone. How was he going to explain what he'd seen when he called his wife?

Here he was, a decorated soldier, a man who had served his country, who had sat through raids and had had spitfire artillery splashing all around him. And now here he sat frozen, a couple yards away from a flock of geese sitting in a circle and acting as passive as Gandhi. He didn't know what to do. Play Duck-Duck-Goose with them?

He started to whistle "London Bridge Is Falling Down." Not one goose lifted its head. He started to sing "Oh When the Saints

Come Marching In" and not one goose lifted its head. Billy decided to stand on his machine and flap his arms, calling out to them in a language he was sure they understood.

"Honk. Honk!" Not one goose lifted its head.

Finally, he jumped off his machine and decided to take a run at them. He put his head down and dug his right foot into the thick Kentucky blue grass and pushed his body forward with his head wrapped inside his tattooed forearms.

"AAARRRRGGGHHH!" he growled, and when he looked up, he saw the geese taking a few steps. They were cluttering his daybreak. He stood in awe as all sixty of them swelled into the beautiful first light canvas of red and soft blue. He felt a tear slip from one eye and sighed.

What a beautiful sight. What a gorgeous start to his day. If he were a religious man, he would have called it a blessing.

His body turned in a slow semi-circle, following the pattern of the wings taking flight. All he could think to do was to applaud the symphony of geese that filled the sunrise. His hands pounded against one another and reached high over his head. A singular standing O. He was in a state of amazement.

Amazed at the beauty of life. Amazed at nature. Amazed and grateful for being alive. He shook his head and uttered a quiet thank you to the sky, smacked his wide palm against his lips and blew a kiss heavenwards. He turned back toward his machine and that was when he saw it. A lump.

A lump curled up in the fetal position. He walked toward the lump and turned on the flashlight app of his phone. A body. Not a lump. A frozen body. It had clearly been lying on the fairway through winter. He stepped carefully toward it.

It wasn't moving. There was no breath rising from the shoulders. There was nothing. He shouted, "Hello?" even though he knew there was no point. No movement. He knew he shouldn't touch it, but he couldn't help himself. He put the toe of his running shoe against the right shoulder of the body and gave it a gentle tap. No movement. Rigor mortis had turned this body into a solid heap of solid decay. He told himself just one more try before he dialed out.

Billy shoved the shoulder hard, hard enough to see that it was a woman's face inside of a black hoodie. He made the call that no one ever wants to make. He dialed 911.

"My name is Major General Billy Townsend. I just found a dead Indigenous woman on the golf course I work at."

"NIGLAHUKTUQ," SHE WHISPERED TO THE DARKNESS. "NIGLAHUKTUQ," she whispered one more time to the cold air, watching her hot breath form a thin, grey poof cloud in front of her nose.

"Pihuktuq!" she reminded herself. Keep walking and walking. She knew that if she stopped, she would sleep. If she slept, she would die.

"Mama!" she called out. "Mama!" No answer came to the cold hill she stood on top of. Not one echo of comfort. She had no one to sleep close to on another minus forty night.

She knew she should have taken that winter coat from the mission. They were giving them away, but she wouldn't take one. She didn't want anything from them. Not since they took her baby away because the people at the mission had told the social worker that she couldn't take care of him. As if a parka could replace her son. Fuck Edmonton. She clamped her hands together inside her hoodie pouch.

She and her mama had fled South on the promise of a white man. They had fled South thinking that they were going to make it. Back home, that's how you made it. You latched onto the arm of a white man and you were set. You had made BINGO! You were off welfare. You had three meals a day on your table. You were never cold, and the only trade-off was becoming their little sex slave. That was the easy part. At first.

She and her mama had left their home for "better days ahead." Something that her mama always said to her. "Bunny, there'll always be better tomorrows. Remember that."

In the cold of this night, looking down at the iced-up North Saskatchewan River, all she could see was the awfulness of all her yesterdays after they had come here in hope of all their better tomorrows. Her mama a woman in love and she a teenage girl wanting to finish high school. Finish high school and go to the big school. The one that was never in the North. The one called university.

But their lives became a tangled web of booze and dope and sleeping on sidewalks together. Spooning like two young kids. Twins wrapped together in an amniotic sac of concrete. One who looked like a slightly older version of the other. They had learned to eat from dumpsters. They had learned to shit on sidewalks. They had learned to give their bodies away to any man who had a bit of money.

They worked the streets together. Sometimes billing themselves out as a Husky Mom and Daughter Tag Team. When they were first new to the city, they became a sensation. They made 95th Street their bedroom. So many guys coming into town from their swing up North in one of the oil camps wanted a reminder of the life they had there. They were the best customers. Loose with their money. Loose with their booze. Loose with their fists.

She and her mama had sported so many black eyes. So many cracked ribs and so much rig pig sperm in their stomachs. Some days that was the only nourishment they had.

When the times were good and the money was flowing from the oilfields into their pockets, they would stay at a hotel that overlooked the river. They'd gaze out the shiny windows and tell each other that this was the life. The life that they were meant to live. This was the city where they would succeed. They would go out for mani-pedis. Get their hair done up good and buy sexy, too-small black dresses. On those stretches the clientele changed to old white men looking for an Eskimo dog sled ride. And they gave it to them.

Hunched on their knees, propped up on their elbows and making sure the sounds of traditional throat whispers came out of their mouths. Singing yelping whispers out into the rooms that were overpriced and overrated, with men in tweed suits shoving themselves into them from behind, doing all the things they would and could never do to their trophy wives.

Old white men, the people she and her mother called utuqqaq, old man. They were an odd group of business partners, millionaires who thought they had hit nirvana when they were in bed with an Eskimo woman. They were finally free to be who they really were when they were mushing the mother and daughter who denied them nothing. They could let loose and hit Viagra-free orgasms. Something they hadn't done at home in years.

As long as the mom and daughter tag team each made enough money to keep paying for their room, they could live the good whore life. They could pretend that what they did was a career. A life that they had control of.

But it wasn't. They told each other that this was the good life but knew that they were only lying to one another. At least their lies boosted their spirits. They gave away their bodies for the safety of a fancy, warm hotel room. A room where they did things to men and to one another that they would never do otherwise. It was survival.

Survival of the fittest, Darwinian law.

Bunny kept walking. She couldn't feel her toes anymore. Knew that frostbite had set in. Nothing mattered. Her toes didn't matter.

Her life didn't matter. She had tried. She had tried to be a good girl. She had stopped all dope and booze and smokes and sex for the full nine months while her little boy grew inside of her. She had gone the right way for the first time in so many wrong-way years. She reminded herself, just keep walking. Don't stop. Don't rest.

Kivgalo and Riita walked on either side of Bunny. Tainna, the unseen ones. Neither of them liked bringing home the young ones. So many of them lately. One after another.

Riita stuck her chin out in front of Bunny. "Kivgalo, I'll walk her across the ice. You go ahead and make us a nice fire." Kivgalo motioned a slight nod. There were days when he hated his job.

BILLY TOWNSEND WAS BECOMING OBSESSED WITH THE GIRL FROM the golf course. Who was she? What did she do? How did she end up on the golf course? Why didn't anyone find her earlier? What the hell went on in this town? Fuck Edmonton.

The cops were no help. Said that she didn't have any ID on her. Nothing. They didn't even know how to find out who she was. No wallet. No purse. And no, they weren't sending sniffer dogs out. Who knew how long she'd been lying there? They kept telling him to think about the bush surrounding the golf course and the river so close by. They'd lose her scent too quickly. Why deploy manpower that was needed on a real murder case? Maybe dead Indigenous women weren't a priority, he thought. As far as they could tell, she wasn't murdered. Let the toxicology results speak for her.

He couldn't wait and he didn't know what to do. He didn't know where to start. He only had the memory of her face and her black hoodie with a weird design on it. Her face, that dull frozen look of dead eyes and the tiny stain of red, a red drip bleached into the corner of her right lip. Billy knew that was blood. Old blood. Very old blood.

He had seen dead faces in his former line of work, but none of them stuck with him the way the young woman's did. When he was at war, the dead faces were casualties. Casualties of their messed-up countries. She a was casualty of Canada. An Indigenous casualty of Canada, but no one cared. Why would they?

He had to find out something about her. The cops weren't moving on it. Billy did what everyone does nowadays. He started looking up hoodies online. It was the only thing he had to go on. Here he was, a decorated soldier—and there was this Indigenous woman with a weird hoodie. He downloaded a picture of a hoodie that looked a bit like hers. He tucked it into his pocket and got into his car. He would start on 95th Street.

SO DARK. SO COLD. IF SHE GOT ACROSS THE RIVER THINGS WOULD be better, Bunny thought. If she got across the river she'd be away from downtown. Away from all of them. The people at The Hope. The people at the Royal Alex. Away from all of them. All those people who hurt her. The people who took him away from her. Her boy. Her baby. Her Adam. When the ancestors sent him to her, she knew he was their gift. The best gift she could imagine, and she talked to him from the moment she knew he was inside of her. Playing and growing and laughing while he did somersaults inside her belly. She loved him before his first breath.

Beside Bunny, Riita nodded her old head, making the flap of her red kerchief bob up and down on the back of her creased neck. She could still remember all the love she had for her babies from long ago, when she was a young mom. Riita tightened her grip on Bunny's elbow. She's breaking, Riita thought. Got to get her to the fire as fast as I can.

Bunny kept remembering. Remembering how the nurse put him onto her chest. She knew her baby knew her. She knew he was taking in her smell, and he would always remember that smell. When she looked at him for the first time, she believed in God. She believed in the beauty of life. She believed in all the good spirits and the ancestors who stood next to her and smiled down at him the way Mary had smiled down at her little boy, Jesus.

It was the first time she ever thanked God for anything. She thanked God for the smell that only a baby can carry. She thanked God for Adam's wrinkled, red face. She thanked God especially for letting her see her son in his first minute of life. She memorized all his tiny, tiny wrinkles. The ancestors who stood next to her and the God of the white people were showing her what her newborn would look like as an old, old man.

"When I am gone and tending the kudlik waiting for him to come back to me, I will recognize him in his old age," she thought. "Newborn babies have the look and wisdom of the old ones. Mothers will always know their child, regardless of age or time or distance in this life and the next. A mother connects to her child in greater ways than what we can see. Moms and babies are the Forever People."

She held on to that. Held on to that moment over and over, and when they came along forty-eight hours later and said that social services were at the hospital to take him away, she didn't want to let go. She started to scream. Adam cried. He cried for her because he knew she was upset before anything started.

Bunny wrestled for her baby. Her body wrestled. Her spirit wrestled. But they were stronger and bigger, and their sloppy white paws reached into that soft baby blanket and snatched him from her. Took him as though he were just a thing. A blob. A job. A number. Something they had to follow through on. He was not Bunny's child anymore. He became nobody's baby.

All those sad memories flooded into her. They hung inside her chest like spiked icicles. She had to keep moving ahead. She had to keep fleeing away from downtown. All that mess. She knew if she crossed the river, she could find Adam on the other side. He had to be there. Only her mother understood the broken heart that she carried. She knew that she wanted him back, and they had made a plan. A plan to cross over together tonight. A plan that Mama had forgotten. Mama had become just another disappointment in her life. Another person who had let her down. Another person with their own agenda.

They had kept a deal since getting tossed out, first from the white man's house and then the upscale hotel. They had been leaving their graffiti tag in the same spot every night. On their wall. The one they called their Wailing Wall. If one of them drew in a tiny nirliq on the east side of the Boyle Street building, that meant they would meet at The Hope. If either of them added eyes to their goose tag, it meant that they were booked. One eye meant overnight, two eyes a two-nighter. It had been their ritual for the last three years. They lived their lives without cellphones. They checked the Wailing Wall in the morning at ten and again at four in the afternoon. They had a system.

Bunny stopped walking and lifted her head high. She thought she could hear her mama calling her to the other side of the river. Some of their people said that the bad spirits came out at night and talked across the sky. But this was not a bad spirit. This was her mama. Fuck walking across on that blue bridge. Bunny turned her frozen toes down the bank of the North Saskatchewan and headed across. She was so sure she could hear her mama whispering to her.

She was sure it was her mama's voice. She was sure of it.

"Bunny! Atii!"

"I'm coming, Mama!"

Riita nodded her head. Kivgalo had issued the signal. Calling out to Bunny meant that the fire was ready.

Billy glanced over to the blonde woman sitting at the bus stop. How did she know?

Smacking her pink bubble gum between her violently red lips, she smiled at him. "It's your hair, baby. Buzz cut. You soldier boys still have the shortest, worst hair in town. I used to take care of a lot of your type."

Billy walked toward her and took note of her spiked white stilettoes. One contained a black sock. The other a white one. Her grease-streaked hair was topped with a crown of artificial roses, looping around her hoop earrings and tied at the back of her head. Perhaps that was a Hooker Halo? He didn't know for sure.

"Well, ma'am, I'm not new in town, but I am looking for a woman."

"You came to the right place, soldier. I am here to serve. Just like you!"

"No, ma'am. Not you and not that. I'm looking for the young woman who wore a hoodie like this one." Billy pulled the picture from the large pocket in his green khaki shorts. "Do you know someone who wore this?"

"Hey, my name is Polly. Shouldn't we get to know each other a bit more before I answer any of your questions?"

The woman's red, red lips smacked hard against her yellow, yellow teeth. Billy took a harder look at her and could see all the freshly scabbed pock marks on her face. Meth Head, he thought. Definitely a Meth Head.

"And how much will that cost me?" Billy asked. He only had a couple of fives in his wallet. I should have gone to the ATM, he thought.

Billy stayed standing in front of her. Shading her eyes with his shadow, Polly looked up at him and pointed her chin toward the Chinese café across the street.

"It'll cost you breakfast. I haven't eaten in a few days."

Billy sat across from Polly, watching her guzzle down a breakfast of sausages and eggs. She was gulping her food. No chewing involved. He wondered how many minutes it would take for her to puke it all up. He had better talk fast.

"Here's the picture again. Have you ever seen a young Indigenous woman wearing this?"

Polly leaned in and a drop of egg yolk dripped from her chin onto the picture.

"Nope!"

"Please look again. One more time and think about it." Billy moved the picture closer to her plate and away from her chin.

"Yep, maybe. Let me see. There was this girl. Ah, I can't remember her name. But she worked along here for a while. We were all jealous of her at first. Her and her mom had pretty much taken over. But the new meat gets old pretty fast on these streets. I don't know where they are now."

"Her mom? What about her mom? Is she still around here?"

"Sometimes I see her at The Hope and sometimes I see her at that fancy hotel. She's all over the place."

"Fancy hotel? Which one?" He was fishing for information.

"You know the one. You soldier boys love going there." Polly managed a grin and the many gaps between her teeth were plugged up with bits of white toast and bacon. Not a pretty sight at breakfast, or ever.

"Thought all you soldier types liked to take your fancy women there to impress them." Polly began to pick the food out from her front teeth with the tine of a fork, scraping the mush from her mouth in sideways swipes. "It's an upscale sort of place to fuck a lady. Gawd, you could do that for so much cheaper in the back of your car!"

"Well, Polly, I'm not going to comment on that, but I think I understand what you're saying. I'll pay for your breakfast and be on my way. Thank you for your help." Billy extended his right hand. Polly placed her right palm in his and intentionally bent and rubbed her middle finger into Billy's palm.

Billy started to pull back his hand, but Polly gripped it a bit harder and smiled up at him, saying, "Remember that I am always here and ready to serve, soldier!" She winked her right eye so hard that her false eyelash fell off and splattered into her plate.

"Damn you soldiers! You always fuck me up!"

Billy smiled at her and tipped his ballcap. "See you again, Polly," he said as he walked out the door.

Billy wondered about the fancy hotel as he got back into his Jeep. He found that hard to believe. He shrugged and started the engine. "Fancy hotel it is!" he said out loud as he burned a U-ie and headed south on 95th Street. He shook his head and started to laugh. Polly's eyelash stuck in egg yolk.

"Fuck me," he muttered.

KIVGALO SAT BY THE CAMPFIRE, WAITING ON THE OTHER SIDE OF the river. He had known her before she was born.

"She's not going to make it," muttered Kivgalo, one of the oldest of the old ones. "Her spirit is too broken."

"I have to protect her though," he muttered. "When I lived, I was a strong hunter and now, in this life, I must give that strength back to The Living Ones. It's my duty, but she won't listen," whispered Kivgalo to the flames. "Her heart is shattered. I've been with her all her short life. Saw how smart she was. How quick her mind could be. I had hope for this one. You know, when they're born and we see their turnik and we know they are different. Different from the others. But she's too broken now. We can die from a broken heart. I know that."

Kivgalo continued talking to the flames. "I loved someone once. Loved that white woman with all my soul. Waited and waited for her to love me back, but she wouldn't. She couldn't. And I had fun with her. Fishing and eating in restaurants and laughing. Our long talks about life and love and how to manage it all. But she couldn't love a Native man. At least not out in public where her friends could see us. One time after a great romp in bed, I asked her, 'Is this all we are?' and she nodded her head. That nod yes was the beginning of my end."

Riita sat down across from Kivgalo and leaned her head back, ran her hand over the red kerchief that wrapped her grey hair in tight. She smacked her toothless gums together and took a deep drag off her cigarette.

"Kivgalo, we both know her heart is broken and it's a bigger break than yours or mine. When she gets here, we'll welcome her. Wrap her up in a blanket. Take her with us. It's best."

Kivgalo stared into the fire. His eyes sad. He never argued with Riita. They had cared for the Living Ones together for decades now. She was always right. She always knew when their time was up. She always knew when hopelessness had locked in. He nodded.

BILLY PARKED HIS CAR AND CROSSED THE ROAD TO THE HOTEL overlooking the river. He had many memories of dropping troops here. There were so many of them during his military years. Polly was not wrong when she said she had taken care of their type. They had been regular customers to more than a few Ladies of the Night. The boys liked having them around. They knew what to do. How to get it done without commitment. No having to say words you would never mean after all of it. Never having to call them the next day. It was a cut and dried business transaction. It was perfect.

He strode up to the doorman and introduced himself. Extending his hand, he said in an authoritative voice, "Hello, I'm Major General Billy Townsend, and I'm hoping you can help me."

The doorman lifted his tired eyes to meet Billy's. I'm so sick of this shit, he thought. So sick of these military types showing up out of nowhere and throwing their rank around like it means something beyond the barracks. Still, he couldn't be rude to the man. He knew there were cameras all over the inside and outside of the building. He knew he was under heavy surveillance.

"How can I help?" the doorman said politely, but all he could think about were the whores these guys dragged through the doors on Remembrance Day each year.

The doorman wished the rest of the country knew what he did. The women he'd seen the servicemen use. The way they talked about getting a whore to break two of the biggest rules of their profession. How they got them to kiss their lips. How they got them to orgasm. Vessels. That's all those women were to them. Hollow containers to be filled. He detested these military types. Men who lived falseness, but who expected everyone to bow down to them once a year and remember that they had given us our freedom.

"I understand there were a couple of women who used to work out of here. I'm looking for them. I've been told that they were Inuit women. A daughter and mom duo. Ever seen someone wearing a hoodie like this?"

Billy put the picture of the hoodie in front of the doorman's eyes. The doorman had seen it before. He had talked with those women. He knew who they were, but why would he help another creep?

"Sorry, sir, I've never seen that hoodie and have no recollection of a couple of Eskimo whores working in our establishment."

Billy leaned in a bit closer. "I was one of their customers, and I need to spend some time with them, if you know what I mean." The doorman felt the familiar squeeze on his left shoulder. Something all these military guys did. Always a physical reaction from men who killed others, men who were put on a pedestal, men who led the dirtiest of lives when they were out of uniform.

He leaned his head close to Billy's right ear. "Listen, you fucking Has-Been, I don't know them. Get the hell outta here before I call security."

Billy stepped back and shook his head. "All right," he said, placing both arms in the air. "No problem, but don't think I won't be back."

Billy got back into his Jeep. Asking people on the streets wasn't getting him anywhere worthwhile. He drove to the police station on 103A Avenue, where the officers who'd come to the golf course had been stationed.

"MAMA! MAMA! NANIITPIT?" BUNNY KNEW SHE WAS GETTING weaker. She felt as though her feet were no longer attached to her ankles. She felt like she was floating around in the air. She felt like a bird. Able to move around without touching the ground. Able to fly.

"Over here! Come sit with us by the fire, my girl." Riita opened her arms to her.

"Where's Mama? I thought I heard her call me." Words tumbled out Bunny's mouth without her controlling them. "Who are you?"

"Here now. You know who I am. I've been with you since you were born. I'm the ancestor who has had the privilege to walk with you over these few years."

"You're a ghost?" Bunny asked but felt herself smile at the same time. Funny to have a ghost walk around the world with you. "Did you see—everything?"

Riita grinned. "You mean the sex parts of your life? I do know when to leave a room." Riita chuckled and offered Bunny a cigarette. Bunny took the cigarette, hoping the glow of the tobacco would hide the redness of embarrassment that seeped up her high cheekbones.

She lit her smoke and felt the warmth of the blanket spread across her shoulders. She felt at ease. She felt something she had not felt in years. She felt safe.

"Where's Mama?" she asked Riita.

"Oh, now we aren't gonna worry about her. We have to take you home."

"We? Who is we?"

Riita pointed across the flames. "Me and him. We're gonna take you somewhere where you'll never be cold again. Where there are blueberries that grow on trees above our heads and where there is always meat to eat. You'll see what a beautiful land it is."

Bunny looked over and saw Kivgalo sitting across from her. He looked calm but sad. He looked like a man she could trust. The first one.

"But Mama and Adam. I have to find both of them. Can I bring my baby with me?"

"No, my girl. Your baby has to stay here."

"How does this work? How do I go to that land?"

Riita stood and held out her hand. Kivgalo was already waiting for her to stand. He reached under both of her shoulders and lifted her up.

"Come with us and you will see, because the best is yet to be," sang Riita.

Bunny stood between her two closest ancestors. Felt the shawl of their protection cloak her shoulders. Felt safe and free. Warm. This is what a smile must feel like, she thought.

She was going to where she could start over again.

"HELLO, THIS IS MAJOR GENERAL BILLY TOWNSEND," HE INTRO-duced himself to the officer on duty. "I found a dead woman on a golf course the other day. I want to know the results of the toxicology report."

They talked a little, then the young officer disappeared. After about ten minutes, he re-emerged from the records room. "The tox screen came back clean as a whistle. Not one milligram of anything inside that woman. What about you—you found out anything?"

Billy cleared his throat, "I found out that she might be an Inuit woman. She and her mom worked 95th for a while and moved their act over to a hotel on the river. I'm trying to find her mom. No luck. Not yet."

The cop looked at Billy. "Who have you been talking to?" he asked.

"Found an old Meth Head on 95th who knew the hoodie she wore. She's the one who told me about their Eskimo road show."

"The investigating officers didn't think of that—the hoodie. We'll put a picture of it in the *Journal*. Hope for a response. Stay in touch, General. We'll let you know." The cop leaned across the desk and Billy shook his hand.

"Thanks, officer. Do stay in touch."

From the police station, Billy went to The Hope Mission. He stood outside the door and watched all the detritus of humanity stroll past him. Billy walked up to the only woman who was standing in the lineup. She was short. Hair cropped close to her skull.

"Hi, I'm Billy and I'm looking for a woman."

The tiny lady looked up at him and grinned. "We all are, soldier," she muttered.

How in hell do they all know! Billy laughed and shook his head. "Not like that. I mean, I'm looking for the girl who wore a hoodie like this." Billy held out the picture of the hoodie.

"That's my girl's hoodie!" said the woman. "Where'd you find it?"

"Come," Billy said. He led the lady off to the side of the chow line. "Are you sure this hoodie belonged to your girl?"

"Yes. Where is she? Haven't seen her in so long, and we always stay in touch at our Wailing Wall. Where is she?"

Billy took both her impish hands into one of his, "Are you her mother?"

"Of course I am. Where is she?"

"Listen, we don't know each other, but I need you to come with me to the cop station. I need you to talk with them. The one on 103A Ave. Will you do that? Or I can call one of them over here to talk with you."

The police came and talked to the woman at The Hope. Billy knew he would never forget the day he watched her scream. Saw the rawest of emotion fall out of her. Saw her slump onto the sidewalk and bang her head on the concrete. The day he saw her mother's blood splash up against the cop car and the young cop grabbing her by her waist and lifting her high into the air. Her heels digging into his shins. Her body finally stopping and her shoulders slumping onto the cops' chest. This was anguish.

He went with her to the station to identify the body. Afterwards they sat together, and she told him the story of the baby. The woman talked about how her girl only needed to be able to see her son. If only they had let her visit with him. Even for just a few hours a week, but no. No. No. That's what had broken her. That's what had stopped her from breathing.

Billy told her that he had found her daughter surrounded by geese. The woman smiled. Told him that it was a good sign. A sign that said she was okay. Off in one of the lands. The geese had protected her body. They wanted her to be found by him. Billy had not one clue what the mom meant.

In time, Bunny became a cold case. No clues. No drugs. No booze. Just another Inuit woman lost inside of too many statistics. No one cared. But Billy had one thing left to do.

IT WAS MIDSUMMER AND BILLY WAS TWIRLING HIS MACHINE AGAIN on the golf course. Little Adam burst into the best of giggles. The kind of sound that only a child can make. The sound that brought a smile to Billy's face. Adam's dark, slanted eyes held tight onto Billy's as the two of them spun around laughing. They were disrupting the morning stillness with their laughter. They were disrupting the morning stillness with their love.

Billy looked down at Adam and reminded him that after their mowing they were going to go visit his anaanatsiaq at The Hope.

"And if we're lucky, maybe your auntie Polly will be there too." Adam smiled up at Billy.

Billy stopped. He held Adam up toward the sky and said, "Look, Adam! Your mama's birds. Nirliq! Geese!"

Riita and Kivgalo stood a few metres away from the father and son. Riita patted Kivgalo's hand and smiled at him. "You did good this time."

Glossary

Ajujuq: Run fast!
Anaana: Mother
Anaanatsiaq: Grandmother
Anirniq: Spirit
Ataatatsiaraaluk: Great-grandfather
Atigi: Caribou parka with fur inside
Atii: Come, come along
Iqaluk: Fish
Irngutaq: Grandchild
Kamik: Skin boot
Ma'na ataatattiaq: Thank you, grandfather
Ma'nallunav'juaq: Thank you very much
Maligaq: Law
Mumiqtuq: Dance
Nananuak: An evil female spirit
Naniitpit: Where are you?
Nauk: No
Niglahuktuq: Cold weather
Nirijuguk: We eat (two people)

Nirliq: Canada goose
Nuliaq: Wife
Patqut: Aged caribou fat and bone marrow
Pihuktuq: (He/she) walks
Qanuitpit: How are you?
Saimmasimaniq: Peace be with all of you
Takuturaunniarvuguk: See you later (some time in the future), alligator
Turnik: Spirit, soul, essence of a person
Tutsiavigvaa: Let us pray
Ubluriaq: Female evil spirit
Utuqqaq: Old man

Source: Inuktut Tusaalanga, Paallirmiutut dialect:
https://tusaalanga.ca/glossary